The Scum of The Earth: Book 2: Bloodlust

Erica Hart

DEDICATION

This is dedicated to those of you who have had to fight
their inner demons.
In the depths of the darkness, always hold onto the light.

CONTENTS

ACKNOWLEDGMENTS

Many thanks to Ash Ericmore for another stellar job on the front cover design. Thank you for bringing my twisted vision to life!

1 TWO LIVES

I rolled over, delighting in the luxurious feeling of Egyptian cotton sheets. Fuck. I was in Adam's bed again. That's the third time this week. My bright idea of using sex to delay the looming decision I had to make was causing me to be more ensnared in this three-way love affair.

Adam had spoilt me rotten. He had bought me this gorgeous pair of light up stripper heels I'd had my eye on and last night he cooked for me. He even let me choose our food.

At dusk, we went for a drive near the lake, and I saw a hot guy jogging with a cool set of silver headphones on. He was wearing a loose vest and shorts and had a tight arse and muscly legs; the moisture of his exertion gave his skin a delicate sheen, making me want to see more of his juices, especially his blood.

"I want him," I breathed, and Adam smiled.

"Fancy some rump steak this evening do you. Whatever you desire Milady." Adam pulled over to the side of the road and popped the hood. I bent seductively over the engine bay, knowing my short skirt was showing a glimpse of my arse. "Try it again, I think it's overheated," I said, and Adam pretended to pump the gas. As expected, the chivalrous jogger couldn't pass by and see a hot girl fumbling with an engine without stopping to help. He pulled off his headphones. "Do you need a hand?" he said, stooping to look under the bonnet, raking his hand through his brown hair. "Yes actually," I grinned, licking my lips, as Adam came behind him and injected his neck, "I'm starving, and you are just the meal I'm looking for." The jogger slid to the floor, and we flung him in the boot.

Back at the house, the hunky jogger was roped to a metal table in the Blood Rooms. We had stripped him naked and now Adam had my head pushed onto the guy's cock, loving seeing it disappear down my throat as he ploughed me with his girth.

"Fuck baby I love seeing you suck cock." He said, his voice thick with want. I could hear my pussy squelch as he went in and out. I was so turned on, I loved having two men at once, I just wished that this other guy was Brian. The jogger awoke groggily, pleasantly shocked by his throbbing member being slurped by my hungry mouth.

"If you'd wanted a threesome, you should have just asked," he mumbled, still disorientated.

"Well, we weren't sure you'd say yes, plus I get off on kidnap fantasies," I purred, as Adam groaned and finished in me. I ran my tongue delicately around the jogger's helmet, then took his cock all the way down, where I bit sharply, quivering as his cock blood filled my mouth. He howled like a banshee, and I bit harder still, wiggling my head from side to side, freeing his dick from his groin. The blood squirted out, covering my face and I began to laugh, lost in the throes of mutilation. I licked the blood and rubbed it on my tits, placing the impressive sausage on the serving tray for later.

Adam put a plastic bag over hot boy's head, and I heard him choke and splutter as he fought for air. His body was writhing, trying to free itself from the ropes. I heard a loud crack as Adam swung a lump hammer at his skull. The bag filled with blood, vomit and bubbling spit. Adam hit him again and he stopped moving. I picked up a bone saw off the table of torture implements and cut off the jogger's hands and feet, letting the spraying blood cover my legs and belly. Adam kissed me, licking the bits of dick skin from the corners of my mouth. "I love seeing you at your purest form," he said, running his hand down my back, "My wild, beautiful cannibal woman." I groped his sticky cock.

"You let the feral part of me out, now I can't get

enough. I ache for slaughter. I can't believe I lived my life in anguish before knowing what it was like to feel at peace. You did that for me Adam, you set me free."

Adam took the bone saw off me and expertly decapitated the guy. I dropped to my knees, under his severed neck, my mouth open, gulping the fountain of blood like some dehydrated wanderer lost in the desert. Adam sliced the torso with a Bowie knife, gutting him like a fish, picking up fistfuls of intestines and depositing them in a steel bucket. I was still in awe when I saw human insides. Organs and guts are so stunning to look at, coated in plasma and warm to the touch, life ebbing out as you take a bite. I plucked the liver out of the cavity and stuffed it in my mouth greedily, hearing my tummy gurgle as I fed it what it wanted.

"Don't be eating too much before dinner. I don't want you to spoil your appetite," said Adam, putting the lungs in plastic tubs in the fridge. I burped as I finished my last mouthful. Adam wheeled the husk to the incinerator, and I filled a bucket with water and bleach ready to expunge the gore.

Ninety minutes later I was slipping into a black silk, backless mini dress, my hair slicked back. I daubed my lips with some deep red gloss and slipped my feet into my new shoes, squealing with delight when they lit up as I walked. I smelt a delicious aroma of onion gravy as I came into the kitchen. Adam was bustling around the stove the top buttons of his shirt undone, his hair disheveled. He looked sexy as fuck, and it was moments like these that made me forget Brian. He saw me out of the corner of his eye and did a double take.

"Fuck me, you look amazing," he said open mouthed. I smiled and said, "Do you need me to do anything?"

"You can open that wine that I've put over there." I turned to see that he had laid the wooden table at the other end of the kitchen, complete with candles and a bottle of red. I poured two glasses, and I had that funny old feeling again. I was happy. Fuck. Why the hell was I scooting to Brian at every chance I got when I had a perfectly hot, perverse guy right here, and he could cook.

Adam pulled my chair out for me, "Allow me madam," he grinned and brought a large golden tureen to the table. It smelled divine. I lifted the lid and saw the jogger's skull bobbing up and down. His skin and flesh had been boiled off and I could see his eyeballs mixed in with the carrots and gravy.

"Dead Head Soup," announced Adam, ladling the mixture into two bowls. This was the first time I'd eaten human meat cooked and fuck me It was good. The meat melted in my mouth.

"I love seeing a girl with an appetite," said Adam, as I ate like my life depended on it, mopping up the remnants with some crusty bread.

The main course was braised cock. Adam presented the phallus with a potato gratin side dish. Jesus! The flavour was like nothing I'd ever experienced. It was a bit chewy in the middle, but I ate it all, getting turned on by the fact that this cock had been in my throat in a different manner a few hours earlier. Feeling a little full, we retired for drinks on the balcony in Adam's bedroom. He lit a cigarette and blew a smoke ring.

"That was possibly the most delicious meal I have ever eaten," I said, standing next to the rail, looking out across the immaculate lawn with its sprinklers going off.

"I can whip up a storm in the kitchen when I put my mind to it," Adam said, his hands on my shoulders.

"You don't need to worry about all this shit that's going to go off in the next few weeks. Kendra can handle it and the fact that Brian's party is before ours means we can up our game and make ours better," I said with false bravado, sipping my whiskey. Fuck I was a proper hard spirits gal these days.

"I have some foreign clients coming over a couple of weeks before the party. They have some business they want to conduct whilst they're here. A Cuban guy, Cesar Moreno who's gonna get us some more UK and overseas contacts and a

Japanese guy, Tao Harumi, a millionaire businessman. Both have bought lots of our product in the past. Will be good to meet them in person. Plus, I think you will be raking the tips in during their stay. I've told them all about my best dancer." I nodded and yawned.

"Come on, let's go to bed," Adam said, draining his glass. I can't remember going to sleep, but now I could feel his tongue encircling my clit. I moaned contentedly and felt the dew leak from my pussy lips.

"Good morning, Beautiful," Adam said as I smiled lazily. He gently pulled my arm to the bed post and tied it with one of his silk ties. He did the same with the other one. "What are you doing?" I said, amused, seeing his stonking morning wood wafting in my face. He spat on my cunt and slowly slid into me. I gasped as he reached the very core of my insides. He rode me slow and deep for a while, telling me how much my pussy drove him crazy and that he wished we could spend all day in bed. Then he pulled out of me, reaching under the bed. He had a plastic tub, which, when opened, contained the jogger's hand. It had begun to stiffen a bit, but Adam bent the fingers how he wanted them and inserted them into my juicy gash. I yelped as he put three, then four fingers in me. I yanked my legs open, enlarging my hole so he could get more in.

"Yes, harder!" I screamed as he inserted the full hand up to the wrist into my welcoming quim. My cunt was streaming with nectar as Adam grabbed my tits and then inserted his throbbing appendage into my enlarged stuffed crack. Fisted by the dead and fucked by the living. We came in unison, and I howled the house down, knowing by now that Adam's staff were used to our loud fucking.

Later in the club, I was still basking in the afterglow of the hot fuck I'd had that morning. My pussy was throbbing as I swung seductively round the pole naked, aside from my light up shoes. I noticed Gladys sitting on one of the tables. Fuck, I knew I was going to have to play nice and humour her. She waved a tanned, scrawny arm at me. I took a deep breath, put on my best seductive smile and walked to her table slowly, letting her see every inch of my body.

"Oh, Melody you gorgeous creature! Please sit and let me order us a bottle." She craned her wrinkled neck, but the waitresses were all crowded around the bar.

"Let me see what the holdup is," I said touching her age spotted hand.

I stalked over. "What the fuck, where's Priscilla?"

"She went in the back fifteen minutes ago and hasn't come out yet, said a brunette waitress with tits like beach balls and whose name fucking escapes me. I went behind the bar to find Priscilla holding a baby and Kendra trying to placate Adam.

"Priscilla you can't bring your child in here. This is an adult establishment. I could be in all kinds of shit if someone finds her here." Adam said, exasperated.

"Calm down Adam, it's fine we can find someone to look after her." soothed Kendra.

"I'm sorry Adam, but I cannae find a babysitter for Alice," replied Priscilla, sheepishly.

"Give me the baby and get back on the floor. We've got customers," I said cradling the tiny bundle. Two grey, beady little eyes stared at me. I gently touched her soft, rosy cheek. I looked up to find Kendra and Adam looking at me and smiling.

"Now who's the mamma," laughed Kendra.

"Shut up!" I said trying to keep a straight face. The little baby snuggled her tiny body into me.

"Keep her out of sight tonight and I'll speak to my staff tomorrow. We can take her home and Bridget can look after her," said Adam, going back onto the floor. Bridget was Adam's head housekeeper. She was in her early sixties and was another one of the few people I liked. She had taught me how to make dirty martinis for the last Blood Rooms party. Fuck, I was getting more accepting of people these days, and I didn't have my murder fantasies as much now. I think that's because I could act out my base fantasies in person. Woohoo, check out friendly me. This niceness had to stop.

"Can you take her? I must get back to Gladys."
Kendra took the baby and smiled tearfully.

"Are you OK?" I said, as she put Alice back into her
carry cot.

"Yes of course love. She just reminds me of
someone from a long time ago." I left the room,
wondering what the fuck that was about.

Gladys had poured me a glass of bubbles and
wanted to book a private dance. Here we fucking
go. I tensed, knowing how much money Adam
made from her; she was one of his best clients.
Once she was comfortably seated, I began to
dance, arching my back and caressing my tits,
feeling the nipples harden. Gladys' eyes were
bugging out of her head and her pursed lips curved
into a lascivious smile showing her porcelain
veneers.

"Come here Melody and let me taste that sticky
pussy of yours." I closed my eyes and lay down on
the leather sofa, feeling the bony fingers open my
lips, dipping into my love pot, her elderly tongue
searching my vaginal canal. I heard her stand and
when I opened my eyes, the crone was stood over
me, her designer skirt pulled up, lowering her
shriveled cunt on to my face. It tasted like soap
mixed with a hint of piss, but as she began to juice
up, it tasted like rot. The dying insides of an old
woman who tried desperately to look young. She
began to murmur my name, grinding on my face

telling me to tongue her cunt deeper. I was on the brink of hurling up when her juice flooded my mouth, and she twitched in the aftermath of her orgasm.

"Fuck, you little spitfire!" Gladys said, handing me an envelope full of crisp fifty-pound notes. "I want you to join me in my room at the next Blood Rooms party." I gave an inopportune grin as she left the room, then I stuck my fingers down my throat and threw up in the bin.

Feeling nauseated, I went the bar and got two whiskey shots which I necked one after the other. Somehow, I could still taste a hint of Gladys' rancid old cunt. Gross.

"Rather you than me," laughed Priscilla, serving Budweiser to Ellis, a hot black guy. He had beautiful teeth and toned arms and he was sweet on Priscilla. He was also a small-time drug dealer. Adam welcomed him into the club to give the clients little lifters.

"Great moves darlin'," he said, calling to Priscilla to pour me another shot.

"Thanks," I said, dying to go in the back and clean up.

"So 'Cilla how come you don't dance?" I knew these two were gonna end up fucking.

"I do in private Ellis, when I'm high," Priscilla

breathed, her grey eyes sparkling.

"Now that can be arranged," Ellis said, slipping her a packet.

"I get off in a couple of hours. Seems a shame to get fucked up alone. Wanna join?" She slipped the packet in her pocket.

"I don't need asking twice," Ellis said, absentmindedly touching his hard on.

Young love in the fucked-up underworld. There is always passion, even in the darkness.

Back at home, after I had seared the very skin off me under a shower that felt about ten thousand fucking degrees, I got in my own bed. I'd left Adam on a Skype call in the lounge with the Cuban guy. I lay wide awake in the darkness, listening, waiting to hear him come upstairs. After about an hour of me staring at the ceiling and sensually stroking my throbbing clit, I heard him quietly open my door. I pretended to be asleep. I felt him lightly brush my forehead with his lips, then he was gone. When I was sure he was in bed, I text Brian to come and pick me up at the crossroads not too far from the house. That's where we had met the last three times I'd sneaked out to see him. I had to make this my last.

I knew I shouldn't be going to him, but a junkie needs her fix and Brian was more addictive to me than crack. I'd never been to his house; he always took me to the club, saying it was more private there. I never questioned him, but perhaps in the grand scheme of things I fucking should have.

He looked so sexy in a tight white vest and ripped jeans. As I slid into his black Range Rover, he kissed me hungrily. "Fuck, I have missed you. I've got something special for us tonight."

All these surprises off two men this week, fuck I'm quite the spoilt little tart. I smiled, groping his already hard cock.

When we got to the club, he told me to close my eyes and led me into the main room.

"Ok you can open them now," he said, feeling my arse.

I gasped. The whole floor around the oval bed was filled with lit candles of all shapes and sizes. The heat and orange glow off them made the club look eerily like the bowels of hell. There, hung from the ceiling on some sort of pulley, was Paul the barman, totally naked. He smiled when he saw me.

"Hey Melody, I've been wanting to play with you for a while now, and Brian has rewarded me for being such a good pet." It was only then I realised that the thick chain choker I always saw him wear was a dog collar. Brian pulled it and it tightened around his neck making him splutter and his cock wag in arousal. A painfully thin girl wearing a PVC French maid outfit appeared from the shadows handing us a glass of Champagne each, then scuttled away as if terrified of Brian's icy, white gaze.

"Come here sexy," said Brain huskily and I went behind Paul to see that his arse was being held open wide with a speculum. Brian had a silver bowl in his hand which, I noticed was full of eyeballs. He began to shove them inside Paul's anal cavity. Paul moaned with pleasure and the precum dribbled from his dick looking like sticky spider webbing. Brian then balled his hand into a fist and began punching Paul's arsehole, smiling sadistically as he heard the squelch of the crushed eyeballs. Paul was swinging haphazardly with each punch, begging for it to be done harder. Eventually Brian withdrew his fist, now covered with obliterated retinas. The goo dribbled out of Paul's arse and Brian removed the speculum, Paul's arse twitching and still gaping.

"Eat, and don't worry he has douched so they won't be any shitty surprises!" The three of us laughed insanely. I bent forward and ate Paul's arse, lapping up the white liquid, hearing him moan for my tongue to go deeper. His dick was rock solid, so I wanked him off whilst I rimmed him into oblivion. I then kissed Brian, spitting the goods into his mouth. Brian lowered Paul down and told me to strip and lay on the bed.

"Since I'm so pleased with you, how about I let you touch my girl?" He led Paul by the collar to the bed. By now my pussy was streaming. Paul was good looking and had a long thin dick, smaller than I was used to by this point, but in the heat of the moment, who is splitting hairs? Paul shoved his fingers in my honey pot and licked them slowly. "She does taste so good like you said Brian," he murmured.

"Right, that's enough," Brain said, sharply, "She's mine. But I will let her suck you. Make him come baby whilst I fuck you." I liked being ordered around, and in Brian's presence I was like a little fuck toy gagging for her next orgasm. I deepthroated Paul, feeling Brian roughly banging me, pulling my hips onto his thick meat. Paul came down my throat and then lay next to me exhausted and dripping in sweat, watching Brian pummel my cunt till he spurted his seed. Paul then went to get a shower leaving us alone. I slipped my dress back on, turned on by the fact that Brian's cum was seeping out of me.

"So, where did you get all the eyeballs, I asked, sipping my champagne.

"From here, take a look." Brian showed me into another room off the main floor which I'd never seen before. It was freezing inside and appeared to be some sort of enormous walk-in fridge. Hung on meat hooks were seven teen girls, their eyeballs gouged out. They were dressed in the same French maid outfits as the girl who served us and were quite fucking dead, some in advanced stages of decay. I heaved.

"Some of my clients want them to already be dead and asked for the eyes to be removed so that the victims can't see what is being done to them, even after death."

We came back to the main floor, and I welcomed the heat from the candles, some of which had burnt out by now.

"I'd love you to come to my opening next week. See if you can get it off work," Brian said, longingly.

"That may be a bit difficult to pull off, but I'll do my best," I lied, knowing full well that Kendra would be working here by then and there was no fucking way I could blow her cover or expose mine.

I was silent as he drove me home. Tonight was so fucking wild. Different to what Adam and I had done. My evil side sung with happiness, whilst the not so evil one was telling me to end this dangerous love affair.

2 KENDRA

I didn't know what to say when Melody asked me what was wrong as I held Priscilla's baby. For a moment she reminded me of my own child; the one my mother cruelly tore from my arms only moments after she was born.

I have always been involved in the adult industry ever since I was fourteen. My mum was a madam in one of the brothels in town. She knew that I was a pretty one. I've always had striking red hair that cascaded down my back and an enviable figure with naturally pert tits. I might have had a bit of help in recent years, but the good foundations were always there.

My mum put me to work as a cum dump whore, plying me with cocaine and alcohol. At the time I didn't think anything of it, but she was pimping me out to the highest bidder. She used to put on

in the bath. I was bleeding from both holes where I'd been taken so hard. When the drugs started to wear off and I said I was in pain, she just gave me more and told me to shut up.

A couple of weeks later, I woke up four days on the run throwing up. I shit myself knowing my mum would go ballistic if she found out I was pregnant, so I hid it for as long as I could.

When she did find out and realised that it was too late for me to get an abortion, she said fuck it we'd get rid of it once it was born. She used it to her advantage, pimping a ready to pop teen to men who had a pregnancy fetish.

The men always smelt like cheap aftershave and alcohol, all old enough to be my dad, some old enough to be my granddad. I felt nothing only hatred for my mother, but I had no choice but to do as she said. She never let me have any of the money I made, so I was trapped, forced to be a spunk receptacle for the perverts of Manchester.

As my due date grew near, mum finally let me rest and stopped pumping me full of drugs. The birth was a difficult one and mum got in some backstreet doctor to help deliver the baby. I screamed the brothel down much to the disdain of my mother who had to apologise to all the clients.

The final push almost made me pass out. The sleazy doctor wrapped the mite in a towel and handed it to me.

A pink cheeked, little girl blinked at me and stopped crying as I cuddled her to my chest.

"I'll take her," snarled my mum and roughly pulled her from my arms, causing her to scream at the top of her lungs.

"No mum, I'll look after her, I promise!"

"You have no business looking after a baby Kendra. I need you to get back to work tomorrow. You're the top earner here and so many men want to fuck you. In a few years once you're legal, the novelty will wear off and I need to make as much out of you now whilst you're in demand. Get to sleep, you're fucking all day tomorrow."

She told the doctor to give me something to knock me out and he licked his lips asking if he could fuck me for free since he'd given his services. Mum chuckled and told him to come back at dinner tomorrow. The last thing I remember was his podgy, B.O ridden frame hunched over me, the beads of sweat running down his pock marked face.

I despised my mother even more after that. I spent my days doped up, living the same waking nightmare over and over. I daydreamed about getting away from this life and not being afraid to go to sleep in case I woke up with some strange man in my bed. After my pregnancy, mum made sure to put me on the pill lest it should happen again. I tried to commit suicide several times, but mum always stuck her fingers down my throat when she found me unresponsive. In the end she had me sleeping in her bed after I'd finished work and locked the door so I couldn't do anything stupid. I'd resigned myself to the fact that this was my life until I met Jeremy.

He was a solicitor who, like all the men before him, wanted to be with a younger girl. He was a distinguished gent, with designer stubble and he always wore silk tailored suits and smoked cigars. The first time we were together changed my life.

He didn't force me into anything but sat next to me on the bed and spoke softly to me, breaking the ice and getting to know me. Of course, in my drug addled state I found it hard to come up with much decent conversation. When it came down to the fucking, he took me gently, almost lovingly and even wore a condom. Afterwards he cuddled me and thanked me for allowing him to be inside me. I had never been treated like that by a man. I was shocked. He quickly became a regular and I found myself looking forward to seeing him. It felt nice to be treated like a person. Granted he was still a pervert, but he made it seem less offensive.

One day my mum came into the bedroom we both now shared and slung a suitcase onto the bed. "Pack your shit, you're leaving," she said, devoid of emotion.

"What do you mean?!" I said, not believing my ears.

"Jeremy has bought you. He's responsible for you now. You're getting a bit old for underage gangbangs anyway. I've made what I can out of you. Get out."

That was the last time I saw my cunt of a mother.

Jeremy had rented a little terrace for me to live in. I was to be his mistress and the dirty secret that he kept from his wife. It gave him pleasure to lavish gifts and affection on me and about a month after I'd moved in, he told me that he loved me. He said he wanted to be with me but couldn't leave his wife. She was something of a socialite and well known among the upper echelons of society, and a scandal like him divorcing her for a younger model just wouldn't do.

Jeremy, I found out, was a filthy prick sexually. He organised exclusive sex parties at my abode, where snooty clients of his would come and fuck, swapping partners and living out their kinky fantasies. He told me I didn't have to fuck anyone that I didn't want to. He just loved hot sex and his wife had about as much passion as a corpse. He wanted me to experiment and find out what I liked since I'd been forced to do things against my will for so long.

Jeremy would fuck literally anything. He especially loved pounding my pussy whilst being fucked up the arse by a well-hung stud. A true hedonist, he made sure that the champagne and drugs were always plentiful. At first, I was a bit hesitant, but after a while I knew none of these people were going to hurt me, they were just toffs who wanted a good time.

"Do you ever worry about your wife finding out about our parties?" I said one evening, as we lay in bed, our bodies moist after an hour of fucking.

"She won't find out. My clients are loyal to me. I keep their secrets, so they will keep mine. I have so much on each of them that I could destroy them if they said anything."

I loved the power Jeremy had. I would love to be in that position one day.

As the years passed, Jeremy put me in charge of the parties and my sexual appetite became ferocious and I matched his, fucking both men and women, but I always felt like something was missing.

I never loved Jeremy, but I loved our lifestyle, and he treated me right. One day when he came to call on me, he was very sombre and not his usual sexually charged, effervescent self. "What's the matter baby?" I said as he poured himself a straight vodka.

"My wife is dying. She's gone into a hospice. They don't think she'll last the week. It's just going to be me and the boy now." He drained his glass. I never really asked Jeremy about his family. I didn't want to know.

"Don't you think you should be with her now instead of here with me?" I said, feeling a bit guilty.

"This is my way-out Kendra. Now we can be together. I'm just annoyed that it's took all these years to finally get rid of the old bitch."

"Fuck Jermey! That's a bit brutal!" I exclaimed.

"I'm just fucking vexed. I'm not going to be able to see you for a couple of weeks until all of this is sorted out and I can't stand being away from you. I fucking adore you." He kissed me, his fingers finding my juicy knub and kneading it just the way I liked it. I gasped as he bent me over the back of the sofa and slammed his erection into me. We fucked for three hours straight until my pussy was raw and I fell asleep in his arms. When I woke, he was gone. I didn't see him or hear from him for a month.

He finally turned up with a moving van and excitedly burst through the front door. "That's it baby!! Now you're officially mine and I'm moving you in!" He picked me up and swung me round, showering my face with kisses.

We got to his house, and I was stunned. It was enormous, in its own grounds with a sweeping driveway. I felt like royalty. Who would have thought that a teenage prostitute would end up living somewhere like this! As we entered the house, a little boy of around nine years old stood at the bottom of the elegant staircase. He was handsome with olive skin and chiseled cheeks. He smiled at me and extended his hand. "Hello Kendra. I'm Adam."

We raised that boy as our own. He told me that I was a better parent to him than his real mother, who had been cold, unloving and strict. Once Adam hit puberty, I caught him cutting himself with a razor blade and licking the wounds.

"Adam, stop that You're going to really hurt yourself." I took the blade off him as he sucked the blood transfixed.

"I can't help it Kendra I like the taste." I mentioned what had happened to Jeremy and he said it was just a one off and not to worry. I was still concerned though. That wasn't normal behaviour for a thirteen-year-old.

Jeremy and I continued our lavish, raunchy parties, made even more elaborate now we could hold them in his house. I began to approach people of power and influence and even asked a couple of celebrities. Adam was allowed to come if he wished. We couldn't discriminate about age where sex was concerned, given our track record. Adam did participate a couple of times, but he looked bored and didn't seem attracted to the older clientele.

"I'm so happy with you darling," said Jeremy one morning in our bedroom as he pulled on his trousers. "Adam loves you so much and our parties are really something." I smiled at him through the mirror as I put on my mascara. Unexpectedly, I heard him cough. I turned as he clutched his chest and fell to the floor. "Fuck! Jeremy! Jeremy! Wake up!" I shook him but he didn't respond, and he had stopped breathing. I rang an ambulance, but I knew before they arrived that he was dead.

Jeremy died of a heart attack. All those years of booze and drugs had finally caught up with him. He left Adam and I everything. I no longer wanted to live in the house. It felt like living in a tomb full of old memories, so I got my own place, telling Adam that he oversaw the estate now and had to be the man of the house.

I found my true calling not long after. Adam rang me and told me to come to the house because he had something to show me. I found him in the dank old basement and what greeted me was far from anything I would have expected. Adam had tied a young girl to a wooden table. She was naked and gagged with rope.

"I can't hide it anymore Kendra. I need to let it out. I can't pretend anymore. When you taste it, you'll understand." He picked up a chainsaw and began cutting the girl's limbs off. She screamed, her mouth opening around the rope gag and blood squirted up in the air as the limbs flew to the floor.

She vomited lumpy blood and her body twitched as the shock and pain coursed through her mangled veins. Adam fell to the floor and began licking the stumps, drinking her warm life force, his erection straining against his pants. He ripped off his clothes and then fucked the pitiful remains of the girl. She was silent now. She had passed. He looked at me as he pumped, the blood covering him. He was grinning. "This is what turns me on Kendra. Unadulterated carnage." I stood, immobile, too dumbfounded to do anything. He groaned contentedly as he spewed his muck into her. He then pulled the rope gag from her mouth and blood and bits of sick leaked out. He yanked her tongue out and cut it off with a scalpel, chowing down on it with gusto. "FUCK!!! Meat, raw meat. I wanted to taste this properly for so long. Watching black market snuff films isn't the same as doing it for real."

I came closer, feeling repulsed but strangely interested in watching Adam mutilate this girl. He used the scalpel again, this time to score a line down her torso. He ripped the cut open and exposed her glossy innards, his arms scarlet as though he was wearing gloves. He grabbed her heart and pulled it out, opening his mouth to catch the drips of blood, licking his lips in delight. He gripped my arm and shoved the heart into my mouth. Startled, I spluttered in terror.

"Eat Kendra. I promise you won't be sorry. I know

you're like me. There's always been something missing. I've seen you at those parties, putting on your game face, smiling and fucking, but your eyes look dead. You're not satisfied, but now you will be."

I took a bite, then another and before I knew it, I'd eaten the lot. I can't explain how I felt the first time I ate a human. It was like I transcended somewhere else; like all the things that had been not quite right had all been fixed. Adam pulled out her intestines and put them in a bucket.

"I've been talking to some people who are into the same thing, and they want product, so I'm going to give it to them, at a premium price of course. We could run a little operation here, providing these rich fuckers what they want and enjoying ourselves in the process. What do you say Kendra, will you help me?" I looked around at the horror in front of me and felt strangely calm.

"Yes. But no babies. I will get the bodies, whilst you get us the contacts. If you're pretty and have the gift of the gab, no one will think you are a threat." We humped the remains upstairs and threw them onto the big open fire in the lounge. The smell was sweet and pungent. I wrinkled my nose.

"First things first, you need to fix up the basement and get an incinerator put in so we can dispose of the bodies." He nodded eagerly. It was installed by the end of that week. Thus began our harvesting business. I became a dab hand at abduction, especially of kids. They got us the most money and their flesh tasted the best.

Adam had a few business plans in mind. He wanted to open a strip bar so he could meet potential clients and conduct business uninterrupted and off the radar, the bonus being that he could look at naked girls. He also wanted to open an exclusive club for people like us and began pimping out the basement with expensive bar furniture and little torture rooms where mutilation could be done in secret.

"I think we're going to need help with the running of the basement." I said as we stood outside the strip club watching the neon sign being installed.

"I'll find someone don't worry. We have a few dancers coming to audition before we open and that's your department mamma." I punched his arm jokingly.

"You cheeky bugger! I hate it that I'm that old! But I will look after the girls."

I remember the first time Adam saw Melody. I knew it was love at first sight. I too thought a lot of the girl. She was a hard worker and she had smarts, gumption and was hard as fuck in a fight. It was even more of a perfect match when we found out that she was one of us. Now we were running this enterprise between us, and the cash, notoriety and praise rolled in.

A couple of weeks ago Adam told me she was the one. He'd told her he loved her, and they were living together but it was all in the weird stage of it not being completely official yet.

"Fuck Adam, you need to ask her to be serious with you and take it to the next level. She's a beautiful girl and so many men want her, especially Brian."

"I fucking wish he was dead," Adam retorted.

"Don't worry. We will take him down. You are the closest thing I have to family. That's why I'm going to go and work for him and find out his weaknesses. He's not taking all we have worked for." Adam hugged me and went back onto the floor, watching Melody gyrating on the pole. They did make a hot couple. I felt like a proud mother.

Brian's club was hard to find, but Dario had given me rough directions off the poster on the dark web. I saw the metal black rose sign and knocked on the door. Brian popped his head out, clearly surprised to see me.

"Kendra, what are you doing here?" He said, ushering me inside. His club was decorated to look like a big dungeon, the total opposite to the Blood Rooms aesthetic.

"I'm looking for a job. I can't work for Adam anymore. He's taking all the glory and paying me less money than I'm worth. He's also going soft, mooning over fucking Melody all the time and not putting effort into creating torturous spectacles like we used to. I need it harder." Brian looked at me and I prayed he would believe my shit.

"Well, I could use a hand with some of the bodies, especially the babies." My stomach churned.

"Of course. I'm good with kids." I smiled flirtatiously, touching his arm. He was so damn attractive, but I had this uneasy feeling when I was in his presence. He unzipped his pants and flopped his semi hard dick out.

"You are hot for an older woman. Great tits. Suck my cock baby and let's have a bit of fun." He pulled a blade out of his pocket and nicked his dick. The blood filled my mouth as I sucked, feeling like that little girl all those years ago being preyed on by reprobates. I steeled my nerve, vowing to take this prick down. There was only room for one big cannibal fish in this Manchester pond.

3 NEW FACES

Adam was a bag of nerves. I'd never seen him this worked up. The international clients had arrived and were coming to the club this evening. He was faffing around, making sure the bar was stocked and everywhere was spotless. He'd bought me a sexy new two piece made from silver chain mail. I'd done my make up dark and smouldering, with bright red lips and had curled my hair. Adam loved my hair wavy and wild. I looked at myself in the full-length mirror, hearing the other dancers twittering in the background as they hurried to get ready. I really missed Kendra; she was so good at all this organisational shit. I turned to face the girls.

"Remember to be on your A game tonight everyone. Smile, flirt and make those tips. The clients this evening are very important to Adam and

the reputation of the club, so give 'em a good time."
I went onto the floor as the music began and the
first customers began coming in. I walked to the bar
and got a shot.

"Jesus, everyone is so tetchy tonight," Priscilla said,
filling my glass.

"Adam just wants to make a good impression.
These guys are worth mega money apparently." I
downed my shot and looked for Adam. He was
talking to Fat Cunt No Neck. Priscilla followed my
gaze, "That Derek is a fucking good tipper. He gave
me fifty quid for flashing him my tits!" she laughed.
So, he was called Derek. Shit, I should really learn
the names of all of the scum bags who came in
here, though I thought my nicknames were more
apt. Adam saw me and blew me a kiss. I pretended
to catch it and put it down the front of my G-string.
He smiled, seductively. Then his look became
serious. He went to the front door, where an exotic
looking group were entering. Adam showed the
three Cuban guys to a table in front of one of the
poles and the Japanese guy went and joined Derek
in one of the booths.

"Melody come over here," called Adam, inviting me
to join the Cuban table. "This is Cesar Moreno,
Pablo and Bartolomé." Cesar took my hand and
kissed it, his thin, silky, black moustache brushing
against my skin. "Encantada," He murmured.
"Adam tells me you are his best girl. Would you
mind giving us a little show on the pole?"

"Of course, Mr. Moreno. It would be my pleasure." I flashed him and his two goons my best flirty smile and got up on the stage. Cesar gave me the fucking creeps. He had black eyes that looked predatory like a shark's. His hair was slicked back and glistened under the club lights. He was thin, but well dressed. He made the hair on the back of my neck stand on end. He seemed to omit this essence of pure evil, even blacker than Brian's darkness. He frightened me. I began grinding on the pole, pulling myself right to the top and then free falling, almost to the point where I nearly smashed my head on the floor, but stopped in the nick of time. The Cubans clapped and whistled, enjoying my performance. I saw Cesar looking at me like he was sizing me up, skinning me alive. It made me feel frozen inside, but I kept my smile painted on and took off my clothes, pushing my pussy in their faces. The song finished and I got down, gratefully accepting the glass of champagne that Cesar handed me.

"Most impressive. I'd like to book you for a private dance for my boys. I would join but whilst I appreciate your talent, sexually you are a little old for me." He smiled, handing me a wad of notes. "Give them whatever they want." Adam looked at my pleading eyes and I nodded curtly and escorted the two goons to one of the rooms, feeling their eyes on my naked body.

They sat, expectantly as I put some music on and

began to dance slowly, caressing my tits and singing along to the song, "*In the land of gods and monsters, I was an angel. Living in the garden of evil...*"

Goon one, Pablo, was quite hot with blonde hair pulled into a ponytail and stubble. Goon two, Bartolomé, had dreadlocks and a long, diagonal scar across his face. Both, like Cesar, were well dressed. They took off their jackets and Pablo got his pulsating cock out.

"Come and suck my dick baby," he uttered, pushing my head hard onto his shaft. After a few thrusts, Bartolomé then grabbed me by the hair and shoved his girthy schlong down my throat. It had a silver ring through the helmet which hit my epiglottis, making me gag a little. They took turns ramming their dicks into my throat, groping my tits.

"Lay down and spread your legs. Let us see that juicy cunt," Pablo bit his lower lip as I lay on the chaise longue and spread my lips wide, opening my gash and lightly caressing my clit till the dew coated my labia.

"MMMM so fucking hot for a white whore. We never played with no white trash before in Cuba," grunted Bartolomé. I was fucking seething, the cheeky cunt. I am not white trash and I sure as hell ain't no two penny ha'penny hooker. He got a gun out from his waistband at the back under his jacket. I closed my legs abruptly.

"Hey now baby, we're not gonna hurt ya, just goin' to have a bit of fun is all," he said, winking at me. Pablo grabbed my arms and held me down, covering my mouth with his hand, whilst Bartolomé sat on my legs, shoving his fingers into my, now dry as fuck, pussy.

"Relax Melody. Feel the erotic sensation of cold metal in your hot little cunt." Bartolomé inserted the barrel of the gun into my quim and fucked me hard with it. I tried to scream, but Pablo's grip over my mouth felt like a metal plate. I knew I couldn't escape so I just lay there still, my tears clouding my vision. I felt powerless and utterly defiled. Pablo's dick quivered above my head. He clearly got off on seeing me at their mercy. The prick would soon shut the fuck up if I had him bound with a red-hot poker up his arse, melting his innards.

Bartolomé stopped fucking me and wanked himself off, licking the pussy juice from the length of the gun barrel. "Ah sweet, sweet English puta." He then rammed the gun back into my swollen gash and pulled the trigger.

I jerked and breathed a sigh of fucking relief when I realised that the gun wasn't loaded. The men sprayed their hot spunk all over me and Pablo relinquished me.

"What the fuck!" I yelled; my eyes raw from crying.

"Relax. We were just fucking with you, though I

would love to see a girl get her cunt blown off," smirked Bartolomé.

"Such a perfect little bitch," Pablo said, and licked a few drops of spunk off my cheek.

They laughed as they dressed and left the room. I punched the wall, feeling angry, upset and blood thirsty. Adam could sit and spin if he thought I was going to degrade myself for these fucking twats. I stalked to the dressing room and Adam, seeing I was upset, followed me in. I began fixing my face and pinning up my hair.

"Are you alright?" he said, red faced.

"No, I'm not fucking alright. I'm not gonna play nice with your band of foreign shit heads so you can make a wad of cash. Fuck that!" I strode, angrily to the shower and began cleaning the sperm off my body.

"I'm sorry. I would never have let them go in there with you if I knew you'd come out like that." He rolled up his shirt sleeves and began soaping my back.

They stuck a gun up my cunt Adam! A fucking gun! And then pulled the trigger! Thank fuck it wasn't loaded or your star slut would be fucking dead."

"Don't be like that baby," he soothed as I vigorously towel dried myself. "Cesar is a very dangerous man. He's an arms dealer back in Cuba and he's here to do some business with the Manchester gangs, hoping to expand all over the UK."

"Good for fucking him!" I said slipping on a see-through red dress. "OK. I will play nice with the cunt and his goons but if they ever do anything like that again I will gut the pricks." With that I marched back onto the floor. Cesar called me over.

"Melody, darling, I am sorry for the behaviour of my ingrate associates. They don't know how to treat a beautiful woman of your calibre," he said, offering me a cigar.

"No thank you. I don't smoke. Don't worry about it." I smiled a sickly sweet, prom queen smile at the group, then breezed off to Derek and the Japanese guy.

"Hey Melody!" wheezed Derek, the fat cunt. I swore he was getting bigger. He waved a waitress over to order us some shots. "I'd like you to meet Tao Harumi, all the way from Yokohama."

"Nice to meet you," I said, sitting down. Tao bowed his head slightly and smiled. His lips were thin, and he had long fangs. His hair was pulled back into a ponytail, and he wore a black suit, and, even inside the club, a pair of sunglasses.

"Tao and I would like you to join us when we come to the next Blood Rooms party. Tao here likes boys, but I like both and I love seeing you get the meat going with your womanly wiles before I mutilate it and make it bleed," Derek chuckled. Fucking Tao was like a mute. Great company. Fuck me. The shots came and we clinked glasses. I then made my exit and got back on the pole at the other end.

A man wearing glasses with lenses thicker than the yellow pages gawked at me, his hand down his pants, as I bent forward showing my pink holes. I glided around the pole, my legs open so he could see my inner sanctum, licking my lips as he handed me some ten-pound notes. I finished dancing and blew him a kiss. Then who should I see but that fucking policeman. He waved me over.

"Melody! Fuck you're looking super sexy tonight," he grinned, salivating as I came closer.

"Look, I've told you I'm not going to fuck you, but if you want a blow job, that's fine," I said, wearily.

"Oh really. And what about the underage staff you have working behind the bar? I recognise that girl. She's the teen whose boyfriend was murdered. I could report this place for child exploitation, and it would be shut quicker than that." He clicked his fingers. I rolled my eyes and saw Cesar and his goons coming towards the table.

"Is this man bothering you?" Cesar said, opening his jacket pocket to show a Magnum 357.

"No Cesar. He was just leaving," I said, glaring at the policeman.

"You'll be sorry Melody, you little cunt!!!" the pig said as he scuttled out. The shift was never ending that night and I was dead on my feet come closing time. Adam had decided to let his distinguished guests and for some reason, Derek, stay for afterhours drinks.

"I'm going to get a taxi Adam I'm shattered," I said, pulling on my jacket.

"Get some rest, and I'll see you in the morning. Thank you for tonight. You were spectacular as always." He kissed me and I stifled a yawn. I walked to the taxi rank and was blissfully unaware of the bony figure who crept from the shadows and hit me over the head. It appears men just couldn't get enough of incapacitating me lately.

When I awoke, my head was throbbing like a train had run over my cranium. When my vision cleared, I saw I was inside some sort of rusty old caravan. It smelt like damp. I tried to move, but when I looked above my head, I saw that I was handcuffed to a metal loop on the caravan wall.

"Ah you're awake, you sexy little slut," the policeman said, viciously grabbing my tit.

"You! What the fuck is this place?" I said, noticing all Polaroids covering the walls of different girls, all bound, some gagged, some with huge dildos shoved up them and some beaten to a pulp.

"This is my "Fuck Nest". Oh, I never kill them. They

don't know I'm a policeman and they don't even see my face with my ski mask on. I knock 'em out and bring them here and fuck them till I've had my fill. I love to make 'em scream and beg me to stop. It makes my cock so fucking hard. If they get unruly, then I give them a clout or two. Once I'm bored of them, I blindfold them and dump them on the side of the road, far away from here. The only reason I got caught last time was because she got a glimpse of me without my mask on. But it was a junkie's word against mine, and who do you think the court believed? Surely, she was mistaken. I am a respectable policeman with many solved cases under my belt. I had to move the caravan to a better location, but they had nothing on me," he said, smugly.

"You sick fucking prick!" I spat, pulling on the cuffs.

"You are never getting out of those. They're police issue. And since you know who I am, you're going to be the first whore that I kill once I've fucked you till your cunt splits." He moved towards me and ripped my thong off and began undoing his pants, releasing his puny knob. I bucked like a mule, trying to kick him in his sunken, grizzled face. He dodged my attacks and rooted around in a kids toybox on the floor. He stood back up slapping a riding crop on his palm with a flourish.

"Now, I think you need taming a little," he sniggered as he struck me across my thighs with the whip. I winced but didn't cry out. I wouldn't give the cunt the satisfaction. He hit me again and again, each time harder than the last, his dick getting more erect by the second. I couldn't move after about thirty minutes of his punishment. Some of the welts were bleeding. I began to laugh and croaked, "Is that all you've got?" His nostrils flared and he whipped me across the face, my cheek splitting. I gasped in pain.

"That'll teach you, you whore. You should respect the law!" he quipped, lowering himself and his pre cum dribbling cock on to my battered frame. He spat crudely on his fingers and inserted them into my pussy, then thrust his cock in me, his fingers opening me wider as he pumped.

"Fuck you're tight you little slag, you're better than I thought. MMM, I love feeling you wrapped around my cock."

"It's a shame I can't feel anything," I growled, spitting blood at him. He whipped me again across my tits, leaving another angry red stripe. He removed his fingers and then plunged them into my arse. I screamed and he grinned, basking in my misery. My arse began to bleed as he brutally fisted it. With every punch, my rage grew, and I couldn't feel the pain anymore. I needed to end this piece of shit. He shivered as he filled me with a teaspoon of jism, then dressed and left the caravan, slamming the door violently. Once I heard him drive away, I pulled at the metal hook, swinging my legs up over my shoulders to add strength. I knew my flexibility as a dancer would come in handy one day. I wriggled, pulled and waggled the hook until, after about a fucking hour the rusty metal panel of the caravan wall broke away. I never had the fucking keys to the handcuffs, so I sat hunched in the corner for what seemed like a fucking lifetime, then I heard his car pull up. He staggered through the door, stinking of alcohol and that's when I slammed his head with the metal panel, hearing his skull crack. He fell face down, the blood streaming from the big gash I'd made. I awkwardly felt around in his pockets for the keys to the handcuffs and thankfully found them. Once I'd undone myself, I put the cuffs on him and dragged him to the boot of the estate Toyota, my body protesting in agony. Once he was safely imprisoned, I went back to the caravan, grimacing at my reflection in the mirror. I looked like I'd been dragged up the motorway. My arse hole was still bleeding. I took every one of the polaroids off the wall and noticed that the dick head had stamped on my fucking phone. I managed to extract the sim card and drove the car back to Adam's; thank fuck it was a fancy new model with a built in sat nav. The location of the caravan was well out of the fucking way. I would never have found my way back home without it.

I drew up to the house and Adam came bolting out.

"Fuck, FUCK! Ah baby you're hurt! Who did this to you?!" He helped me out of the car.

"He's in the boot. I want him to suffer. Let's take

him downstairs." Adam was astounded when I opened the boot and he saw the skinny pig in cuffs. We lugged him downstairs and tied him to one of the tables. I threw a bucket of freezing water over his head and put the kettle on. He spluttered and groaned.

"AAAHH! My head!!! Where the fuck am I? What happened?" He mumbled, still under the influence.

"Now it's my turn to teach you some manners you perverted fucking prick!!" I said, my voice oozing venom.

"Do you think you can end me!!??? I am a police officer! No one will believe a filthy slut who gets her gash out for money!" Adam back handed him, knocking out a couple of his teeth.

"Oh, we will not only end you. You will be erased," Adam snarled, his eyes flashing with anger. The kettle clicked off and I poured the steaming water all over the policeman's shriveled cock. He wailed as the dick skin bubbled and split and his bollocks blistered and burst. I then picked up a cheese grater that had been left on the trolley and barbarically grated his cock, watching it disintegrate into chunks. The blood spurted all over me and I was lost in the revenge mutilation, loving every second of inflicting pain on this worthless sack of skin. He was whimpering like a wounded animal, and the blood and saliva leaked from his whining mouth. I ground his dick till there was nothing left and put the remains in a cup.

"I'm done. I don't want to play with this cunt. Let's burn him," I said, adamantly.

"With pleasure," Adam said, and we wheeled him to the incinerator.

"Let me go you twats! You will be locked away for good when they find out what you've done!" shouted the policeman, frightened.

"No one will give a fuck about a crooked rapist policeman. I hope you feel every inch of your skin being burnt off," I said, evilly as we pushed him into the flames and closed the door, muffling his agonising howls.

Thirty minutes later, I sat on the floor of the shower, letting the warm water soothe my wounds. Fortunately, the cut on my face was superficial, Adam said, and should heal without a mark. I felt exhausted and vulnerable. Being a hard bitch takes its toll. The tears came then, and I let it all out; the turmoil of choosing between Adam and Brian, the kidnapping by the four shit heads, the fact I'd just been raped and the countless grotesque men that I'd had to entertain when I would rather have killed them on the spot. Adam had slipped into my room, undressed and joined me in the shower. He sat on the wet floor cradling me as my shoulders shook.

"Ssssh, it's OK, you're safe now. It's over." He kissed my wet head and I snuggled into his naked body.

"It will never be over. There will always be another battle to face. But I'm ready. I just need to get it all out sometimes, so I don't explode." We kissed and he gently washed me.

"Don't forget to drop my parcel off tomorrow," I said as we dried ourselves.

"I won't. What is it?"

"It's the remains of that detective's dick. I checked his wallet. His driving licence said his name was Peterson. I put in all the Polaroids of those girls that I found in that caravan too, and a note."

"What did you put on the note?" Adam asked, putting iodine on my cuts.

"Peterson's past has caught up with him. He got what he deserved. Payback is a bitch."

Adam smiled and delicately kissed my cheek.

4 CESAR MORENO

I always had a hunger for virgin coño after I tried it for the first time back in my twenties, when I was first starting to make a name for myself moving weapons from Cuba to the mainland. I had heard men in the trafficking trade talk about rich clients that they sold niños to, who raped and ate them, believing that the flesh of a child was pure and would grant them youth and vitality. Their stories caused a stirring between my legs. I was a handsome, virile hombre and had no shortage of putas who wanted to fuck me, but their pussys didn't fulfil my longing for something more; something forbidden. I spoke to one of the men and he gave me an address and told me to be there just after dark two days later.

It was just after dusk, and I made my way through

I eventually had to move the bunker to an underground haven under my house. The authorities were sniffing around, watching my every move. No one knew where I lived aside from my workers, who kept quiet because they were terrified, and my men. There, I kept the skulls of all my kills, neatly displayed on a shelf.

It was becoming increasingly difficult to operate my arms business, let alone kidnap niños for my horrific hunger. I knew I was going to have to expand and set my sights on foreign isles.

I'd discovered Adam's harvesting business whilst browsing the dark web. I was ecstatic that I could order what I wanted without having the hassle of procuring the meat. Adam and I set up a secure shipping route, where each member of the chain was paid an extortionate amount of money to make sure that the parcel arrived unopened and in one piece. It was worth every penny. The meat was delicious and tasted different to Cuban niños. Adam told me about his club, where he could get me a child and I could do what I wanted in peace. I decided to pay him a visit whilst also connecting with some English higo de putas about trading weapons in the UK.

I liked Adam's club and his whore Melody had kept my boys entertained, though I warned them about overstepping the mark. These people weren't poor street kids, they were powerful players of the English underworld. Surprisingly, I even warmed to

Tao. He didn't say much, but his brother was a member of the yakuza, and he was a corporate banker. I loved people with disposable income that walked on the shadier side of life.

Adam told me about his rival Brian.

"That cabron sounds a piece of work. But we are here if you need back up. In fact, I may spend longer in the UK. I like it and your white sluts are so much more willing than Cuban putas." I handed Adam a case with a gold Glock 43 inside. "This is for you; a gift for all of the pleasure and good business you have given me over the last couple of years."

"Thank you, Cesar. I will put it to good use, ideally by putting a bullet through Brian's skull." Adam clinked my glass, and I drained my champagne.

I felt horny, so rang my contact asking for some whores, in particular a niña for me. He gave me an address of a brothel where I could meet him. We left Enchant and headed for the whorehouse which was down a seedy back street. I knocked and he opened the door, looking worse for wear. High on something I imagined. I gave him a handful of cash.

"This should cover it. We want to do anything we like, no questions asked," I said as he led us into a large lounge type room with gaudy red and gold velvet furniture and pink neon lip lights on the walls. The man rubbed his raw nose. "Make yourselves comfortable. I will be back in a minute." I sat down and lit a cigar. The corpse like thug returned with a silver tray full of cut lines, a bottle of whiskey, a bottle of vodka and some glasses. A red headed puta followed behind and Mon Dios, a pretty teen for me, all done up with too much make up and eyelashes and slutty lingerie. She looked like a child trying on her mother's clothes. It made me hard straight away.

"If you need anything, I'm just down the hall," said the thug, itching his swollen eyes. The young girl smiled at me and took off her bra, showing her barely formed tits.

"Ah relax," I said, "Let's have a drink first." The teen took the glass of neat vodka and drained it. I saw Pablo put something in the red head's drink. The teen got on her knees and unzipped me, tonguing my polla with finesse. The red head was giggling as the boys pawed her tits and nibbled her neck.

"Lay down and open your legs. Let me taste your pussy," I grunted, and the little puta spread her lips, fingering herself.

"Do you like my cunt daddy? Do you want to fuck me?" she said, licking her cunt juice off her fingers.

"Si, very much," I replied, blowing cigar smoke in her face. I licked her ripe little clit gently, feeling her tremble, then I shoved the lit cigar deep into her tight gash, getting more aroused the more I heard her scream. She tried to scramble away but I punched her in the stomach, and she fell to the floor breathless. I looked at the boys. The red head was slumped unconscious over the sofa, and they were slashing her body to ribbons with pocketknives. They never ate their victims like me, but they loved to hurt women. I turned the teen over and fucked her culo till she shit herself all over me and I filled her hole with my juice. Undeterred, I spun her back over and opened her legs wide and spat on her pussy with a mouthful of vodka. Then I dined on the gash till I was satiated. Her screaming had lowered to a low, whimper as I swallowed mouthfuls of her delectable blood. Fuck, it had been so long since I'd played with live meat. I felt exhilarated. The blood was splattered all over the room. The boys were now double penetrating the mutilated body of the red head, her blood spraying as they pumped. I moved up the girl's body and consumed her little tits, tearing the meat off with my teeth, shivering as I swallowed. I began to pull the skin away around the bite marks, like I was opening a present. My reward was her slimy torso. Delicious. I chomped at the meat of her ribcage until I got to the bones. I burped loudly, full and satisfied. The boys were laughing hysterically. Bartolomé put his gun up the slut's gash and fired. Intestines, bits of stomach and cunt were all over the room. I smiled, revelling in the sheer ferociousness of it all. I opened the door and called the cabron, who vomited when he saw the carnage.

"Now please can you show us where we can shower? And remember to tell the others we have our meeting in two days, and that if they cross me or give us any problems whilst we are here, then a much worse fate will await them. This is us when we are having pleasure. Imagine what we will do if it's to inflict pain." The man nodded, shaking like a rabid street dog and showed us to the bathroom.

.

5 TAO HARUMI

I have always had to hide the fact that I was gay. When your brother is in the Yakuza, there's no way you could disrespect him by saying you like cock. So, I see rent boys in secret, sucking and slitting their scrumptious penises. I tend to pick up streetwalkers and drifters that no one will miss. I handcuff them, being playful and tempting them with money until they have no escape. Then the fun starts. I slice the dick along the shaft in several places and peel the skin back like a banana. The screams by this point are ear piercing, but I don't hear them since I normally wear my ear buds and listen to opera whilst I torture. I find words so tedious when actions have more impact. I love to take my time gorging on the squishy dick meat, longing to feel a dick in my ass, but still waiting to find the right guy to do it. If they are still alive by then, I either cling film their face and suffocate them, or inject them with household bleach, depending on what's available. A lot of the street boys need money for heroin, so often there are needles lying around. I then like to play with their asses as their life ebbs away, finding it strangely poetic that I'm anally raping them with my fist whilst their soul slips from its mortal coil.

My brother keeps trying to get me to join the Yakuza, but I'm happy working at the bank and would rather bludgeon for pleasure not business.

I really like Adam. I think he is a very good host and cares for his clients, putting their needs and enjoyment first. I find his woman Melody very brash. Normal women in Japan aren't like that. She could almost pass for being in the Yakuza, she is very hard and cold, but deals with customers well. I'm guessing she could hold her own in a fight. Fat Derek is an amiable man. I respect him because he is so fucked up and understands my need for cock meat and the butchery of boys. I can't stand Cesar. I find him very loud, arrogant and unprofessional. The way he conducts business and has his goons upsetting the people who are showing him their hospitality, leaves a bitter taste in my mouth. But I pretend I like him to save face until the time arises where I need to cut him down to size. I'd also heard about the other torture club opening at the weekend and discovered through the gossip on the dark web that Adam and the other owner Brian, hated each other's guts. Perhaps I could get rid of this chancer and have a meal in the process. I did like England so far and I may even consider transferring. I have spied so many wonderful specimens on the street since I got here. So much virile flesh to mangle.

I gazed around the busy strip bar. The smell of arousal, money and desperation was overwhelming.

"So, you looking for any cock in particular," said Derek, shoving a handful of peanuts in his mouth.

"I will know when I see it," I said, taking a sip of my cognac and almost choked on it when, as if the stars had aligned, there he was. A young muscular, black youth. He sat at the bar and made eyes at the barmaid. Derek looked at me and grinned, "Ah Ellis. He's sweet on Priscilla behind the bar. He sells drugs if you want some. I don't know if he's into boys though and you're not going to be able to kill him. He gets Adam all his party favours, so he kind of works here."

"I don't want to kill him," I whispered, "I want him to fuck my arsehole." Derek laughed loudly.

"Well go on then, ask him. Can't know if you don't pop the question!" Derek spluttered, sending bits of nuts onto the table. I went to the bar.

"Hello Ellis. I heard you are the one I speak to if I want something." I bared my fangs, feeling lightheaded in the presence of such a beautiful boy.

"Sure man, I got everything apart from meth and heroin this evening. What's your poison?" His teeth were blindingly white, and I felt my ass gape wanting his girth in it.

"I'll take some coke please." I slipped him some notes and he handed me a bag. I ordered some shots of vodka for the three of us.

"You wanna see my tits, for a tip of course," giggled Priscilla.

"Actually, I'm more interested in your friend here. Do you like boys?" The barmaid howled with laughter and Ellis grinned.

"He sure as hell wasn't thinking about men when he was balls deep in my cunt last night!" she said, shooting him a sexually charged glance.

"Aw man I'm flattered, but I don't swing that way," he said, shooting down my hopes of having my ass broken for the first time. I never give up and he was now firmly in my sights.

It was late when I got back to my hotel. I undressed and removed the codpiece with the fake dick attached. It had begun to chafe. I looked down at the remains of my penis; the minute stump of cock tissue left behind after my brother had severed my penis off when he found out I liked boys. I rubbed it thinking about the black youth. I felt the echoes of an orgasm and drifted off to sleep imagining thick black cocks ramming into my ass.

6 PRISCILLA

I opened the door and took Ellis' hand.

"Sweet digs," he said impressed by the beautifully furnished little terrace.

"My boyfriend got us it. He's dead now- murdered. They still haven't found out who did it," I said turning the lamps on and switching on the radio.

"Do you miss him?" Ellis asked, sitting on the pulpy sofa.

"Yeah. He's the father of my wee lassie. But I don't dwell on shit that's happened. What's the fucking point? I just get fucked up to deal with the pain." Ellis cut us some lines.

"Fuck your coke is good." I said, snorting a second

line and beginning to dance and take off my clothes, throwing them in Ellis' direction. I was so wet. I missed having a cock in me.

"*Give me a reason to love you. Give me a reason to be a woman…*" I sang as I seductively pulled down my knickers and dipped my fingers into my dripping cunt.

"Fuck you're certainly all woman to me. I knew you'd be a good dancer. You should get up on that pole. You'd make a fortune," Ellis mumbled. I could see the outline of his big, hard dick through his pants. I pulled his beautiful penis out. It was thick and looked like a polished wooden baton. I shoved it all the way down my throat, fingering myself as I tasted his gluey precum. Ellis moaned with delight, "Fuck you didn't even gag!" He said, amazed.

"When I'm this hungry I won't," I said, lighting a joint and teasing him, rubbing my clit and thrusting in front of him. Then I stumped the blunt out on his shaft.

"Yo, what are you doing?" He exclaimed, jumping out of the chair.

"Bill and I used to get fucked up and have torture sex. It's fucking better than normal sex, I guarantee it. Just relax and be at one with the pain baby. Let it turn you on." I began deepthroating him again, and his wilted dick became rock solid once more. I slid his twelve-inch member into my starving cunt and rode him like he was the last man on Earth.

"MMM, I love big dicks. I love the feeling of being split in half. Put your hands around my neck and squeeze." Ellis gingerly half choked me.

"Harder!" I rasped, "Make it hurt!"

"Fuck me, you're crazy! But that's why I like you." Ellis said, tightening his grip. I grabbed his fingers and made them crush my throat. I started going purple, throwing myself violently onto his cock. Just as I was about to pass out, I pulled his fingers off and squirted my hot cunt juice all over him, coating his tight abs in my secretions. He dug his dick so deep I felt like it was in my stomach as he filled my cavity with his milky jism.

"Fuck that was what I fucking needed. You're learning. Next time you'll know how hard I like it," I said kissing his velvet lips.

"I might have to go out after. I gotta drop off some gear," he said, cutting the last of the bag.

"Bill and I used to run drugs back in Glasgow. We had a good thing goin', right under his boss's nose. Do you know, you' cannae make money working for someone else. You should go out on your own, instead of doing all the donkey work and giving all the money to some prick." I began gently wanking him off, keen to have my cunt filled by black cock again. Ellis murmured, contentedly.

"Fuckin' hell you are a horny bitch!" he said, fingering my cum filled cunt.

"Bite my pussy lips," I said, laying on the floor and opening my legs wide. Ellis obeyed. It made me feel so powerful to have men under my spell; to make them act like me and let them see that the wicked side is better. "That's it, pierce the skin and taste me," I moaned, as Ellis licked my bloody gash. He mounted me, the vag blood and sperm concoction coating his cock like some perverse lubricant. He rammed me hard, spurred on by my teeth in his shoulder. The orgasm nearly made me faint.

A couple of hours later, we went to drop off drugs. It was all going smoothly until we stopped at a house with boarded up windows. The street was a shit hole, full of piles of rubbish and random pieces of furniture left on the curb. The streetlamps were all out apart from one at the far end of the street, so Ellis had to use the torch on his phone to see where we going.

"Be careful in here. This Polish dude is out of it most of the time and can be violent if he feels threatened. Don't say anything. Just smile," warned Ellis, rapping on the door. An enormous man opened the door with a thick ring through his nose. He was over six foot with a buzz cut and wild unblinking eyes.

"Ellis, come in. Who's this?" he said, shooting me a

vile look.

"She's cool. I can vouch for her," Ellis smiled. The man appeared to think about it, then let us in. He reminded me of Bill in a way. I felt a sudden painful pang of loss but pushed it away quickly. Ellis handed the meat head a package and took the roll of money. He counted it and then his face scowled.

"Yo Aleksy, your roll is short. This is the second time I've had to pull you up about it. You know I can get into shit for this. Tareec will bust my balls and I ain't getting a beating 'cause of you." Ellis gently pushed me away from the pair of them.

"Tareec can suck my Polish cock. I'm a good customer. I'll give you it when I have it."

"It don't work like that man. You've got the goods, so you need to pay."

"Oh really!" Aleksy sneered, pulling out a switchblade.

"Fuck this!" I said, grabbing a beer bottle from the table and smashing it. I leapt like a singed cat and jumped on Aleksy's back, jabbing the broken bottle into his neck, where it eventually got stuck. He stared at me incredulously as his pitiful existence was snuffed out. The blood spouted in the air covering me and I felt dizzy with happiness. I picked up the blood-spattered package of drugs and handed it to Ellis, who stood open mouthed.

"Jesus Christ! How old are you again?" he said in wonder.

"Just turned sixteen. Don't be so shocked. I've been on the streets since I was eleven. You grow up fast when you cannae trust no one and have to have your own back. Let's go. I'm hungry. You wanna get some pizza?" Ellis, still agog, followed me out of the house.

"Fuck me you can eat," Ellis laughed, as I stuffed another piece of pizza in my mouth.

"Fucking and killing works up an appetite," I said, between bites. "I love hurting people. That's what makes me feel alive. Now you know. Do you still wanna be here or are you gonna do a runner?" I said, swigging Jack Daniels neat from the bottle.

"Tonight, you've shown me things that I have never seen, especially from someone so young. You've fucking amazed me 'Cilla. I have never felt more turned on, repulsed and shocked all at once by anyone in my life."

"So, you wanna sleep over? My baby is at Adam's till the morning." As I lowered my tight arsehole onto his dick, I knew sleep was the last thing we'd be getting.

The next night, everyone was on edge in work because Adam had these fancy clients coming. I was still basking in the after-effects of the amazing night of fucking and mutilation I'd had. The Cuban guy Cesar was a creep. He made my skin want to fall off. He kept looking at me and smiling, raising his glass. I'd seen men like him on the streets. Pervy cunts who liked young lassies. If he came near me, I'd cut him. The Japanese guy, Tao seemed OK. He didn't say fuck all but was very polite and looked exotic and rich.

Derek kept asking me to show him my cunt. "Derek I can't it's busy in here tonight," I laughed, used to him by now. He was a filthy prick, but harmless really.

"Aw come on Priscilla," he said, staggering a little. I told him to come behind the bar and get on his knees where he wouldn't be seen. He sunk to the floor, his belly spreading like a bean bag as he crouched. I lifted my skirt and pulled my knickers to the side.

"Such a gorgeous cunt. If you let me stick my fingers in it, I'll give you two hundred quid," he said, his voice heavy with lust.

"OK but be quick. I don't wanna get into shit." He shoved his stubby fingers into my twat. I was dry as, but it didn't seem to bother him.

"You're pussy is tight considering you've just had a

sprog!" he guffawed. He licked his lips and handed me some notes. I had to help him up. He waddled back to his booth, sniffing his fingers. Ellis breezed in then, all smiles.

"Hey gorgeous," he said kissing me deeply.

"Hope you've had no bother tonight," I said opening a Budweiser for him.

"Nah, I'm not getting into any shit without my security with me," he winked, taking a swig of his beer. "So, you want to chill after work?" he said, looking at my crotch longingly.

"I can't tonight. They're having some sort of after party for these rich cunts. But tomorrow yes. And I'm sure I can give you a taster when I go on my break." I bit my lower lip batting my lashes at him. I knew he was hard. Just then, Tao came to the bar, asking for drugs. He ordered us some shots and then came on to Ellis! I nearly choked! I would never have taken him for a gay boy.

"I guess I have competition," I laughed, as he walked away. I called one of the topless waitresses over to man the bar whilst I dragged Ellis outside for my cigarette break.

"Where are we going?" he said, as I pulled him behind the bins.

"It's not a cigarette I want to smoke," I breathed, as I undid his fly and swallowed him.

The next morning, I was tired as I rocked up to Adam's. He sent me a cab every morning, which he paid for. I knew I'd landed on my feet since I'd moved here. I'd lost my man but gained some people who I thought I could actually trust for once.

"Hey, Bridget," I said, as Adam's housekeeper opened the door. "I hope she was good last night."

"She was a little angel. She slept right through," Bridget said, showing me in.

"Where is everyone?" I asked, looking around.

"They're in Melody's room. I warn you it's not pretty," she said, sadly. I went upstairs and knocked on Melody's bedroom door.

"Come in," said Adam. Kendra was there too and, lay in bed was Melody who was beaten to fuck.

"Oh my God, what happened?!" I exclaimed, hugging Melody, gently.

"I'm OK, the culprit was dealt with. I should be fighting fit in a few days," she said, smiling painfully. I thought Melody was a bad ass. She was firm, but fair and she stood no shit.

"You're not rushing back to work until you're better," said Adam, looking drained.

"Where have you been Kendra, I've missed you," I

said, squeezing her tightly. She really was like a mother to all of us and everyone felt a bit lost without her at the club, even though Melody was doing a good job at trying to fill her shoes.

"I've had another assignment I've had to work on, but don't fret love, I'll be back at Enchant soon," Kendra said, running her fingers through her fiery hair.

"Just so you know Melody, If I see anyone beating you again I will slit their throat," I said defiantly. "I'm no stranger to defending myself. I did it plenty in Glasgow. I killed a drug dealer once who was trying to hurt me and I loved it," I said dreamily.

The three of them looked at each other.

"So, you aren't shocked by blood and brutality?" Adam asked.

"Fuck no! I recently got reacquainted with it since I moved here and realised how much I've missed it. My man and I loved getting fucked and indulging our bloodlust. Is that bad? I'm not sacked for being weird am I?"

Kendra laughed and looked at Adam knowingly. "The three of us are weird, and there's a lot that goes on that you don't know about, but I had a feeling you'd be a good fit when I took you on," she said, lighting a fag.

"Do you want to earn some extra cash and let off

steam in the process?" Adam asked.

"Always!" I laughed.

"Then come with us downstairs." The four of us went into the basement, Melody linking Kendra's arm, determined not to limp. I couldn't believe my eyes. It was an expensively decorated room with a cage hanging from the ceiling, a cool looking bar and glamorous seating.

"This is the Blood Rooms," said Adam proudly, "A private club where the rich and deviant come to live out their torture fantasies in private. We could do with some help on the bar and, when we get the donors in here, help with keeping them sedated and clean until the party."

"The three of us partake in the eating of human flesh, though you don't necessarily have to Priscilla," said Kendra, stubbing out her cigarette in an ashtray on the end of the bar.

"I've never done that. I just like to kill," I said, feeling my cunt juice up at the thought of it. I would love to play with Ellis in here. "Shit, I've just fucking remembered. Bill told me about this place! He'd seen the advert on the dark web and was gonna bring me."

"Your boyfriend was called Bill?" piped up Melody.

"Yes, here I have a picture on my keyring." I showed Melody the photo of Bill and I looking totally fucked up when we went to a club last New Year's Eve and a girl was taking pictures which you could have made into a keyring. That was the only photo I had of him. Melody went white.

"I think I need to go and lay down," she said, and went back upstairs. I felt sorry for her. The poor bitch must be in agony. Little did I know the real reason behind her departure.

7 THE BLACK ROSE

I felt good that we now had Priscilla on board. I didn't feel as guilty leaving everything to Adam and Melody. I watched as Melody walked slowly back upstairs. I knew she was in agony, but she'd never complain or show it. That girl was unbreakable and reminded me of myself back in the old days when I had to endure so much shit from my mother. Priscilla was a tough little cow as well for her years. She was busying herself behind the bar cleaning down the bottles and putting them back on the shelves.

"So, how's it been?" asked Adam.

"Slow. Every time I try and pick the lock to the tall filing cabinet he has in his office, he comes in. I feel like he senses what I'm doing; it's fucking weird," I said, disappointed. "I've had to fuck him a lot, which isn't a bad thing I guess, considering he's easy on the eye. Shit, I'm having more sex than I had in my youth!" I went to the bar and poured three whiskeys.

"Mama Kendra has good taste!" laughed Priscilla as we clinked glasses. "Adam, do you mind if I smoke a joint?" she said, sitting down at one of the tables.

"No, go ahead," he said, and she dialled a number on her phone and began talking in hushed, seductive whispers. On the phone to her lover no doubt.

"I have a list of all of Brian's clients. They aren't people we have ever dealt with. They read like the inmates of a mental asylum, I'm talking infanticide, demonology and necrophilia, it's pretty heavy shit. I know that Brian has installed cameras to record it all and put it on the dark web to whet the appetites of the morally insane. It's all going to be happening in one big room, not privately like we do it. It's going to be sensory overload," I let out a long breath.

"I appreciate you doing this for us Kendra," Adam said, leaning against the bar.

"Well, it's for our brand and business and these people aren't respectable like our clients. They're dangerous. I know people come to essentially kill and eat their victims here, but they go back to living a normal life, only indulging their debauched desires every so often. I get a feeling that these people who are coming to Brian's club live their lives beyond any code or rules. They are just unadulterated evil. He took great pleasure in giving me the backstory of all of them. I still think there is something that he is hiding. That's why I need to get into that fucking filing cabinet," I lit another cigarette, cursing as it was my last one. I'd have to stop at a garage on the way home.

"Any sign of danger then ring me or Dario. He will come to you any time of day or night. He hates Brain as much as I do and wants to see him scrubbed out," Adam drained his glass.

"One last thing before I go. In his office, there are some pictures of him and another boy when they were both younger. Maybe he has a brother. They are stood with a woman, who is probably their mother. She looks strangely familiar. I don't know if that's significant, but maybe it's worth looking into. We could use it as leverage. Kidnap the brother perhaps, or, if he hates Brian too, then he can be our ally."

"Who's Brian?" Priscilla asked, finishing up her phone call.

"A rival who is opening a club similar to this in a couple of days," I said.

"OOHH are we going to take him down? Can I stab him?!" she said, excitedly.

"Perhaps," laughed Adam, "One way or another he

won't be around long. Shall we all go and get breakfast? I'll get Bridget to make us some eggs Benedict and you can give Alice her bottle."

"Fuck yeah. I'm starving," Priscilla said, taking the stairs two at a time.

The last thing I wanted to do was eat; my stomach was in knots, but I knew I was going to need all the strength I could get for what was coming.

Before I left Adam's I went and checked on Melody. She was propped up in bed by a multitude of pillows, delicately nibbling on a piece of toast.

"Can't this shit hurry up and be over so we can go back to normal? Being you is so fucking hard!" Melody laughed, wincing and holding her side.

"I'm so glad you disposed of the prick who did this to you," I said, sitting on the end of the bed.

"Can I speak to you about something? It's driving me fucking mental," Melody said, sipping her tea.

"Of course, love. You know you can tell me anything. Fuck's sake you and Adam are family to me; like the kids I never had." I suddenly felt tearful and wasn't sure why.

"You know Adam and I have a thing going on, and we haven't made anything official yet. But-" she paused, "if I tell you this please don't say anything Adam will you?"

"I won't I promise. Now spit it out girl." I said, jokingly.

"I've been seeing Brian as well on the sly. I know how Adam feels about him, but I can't help it. I can't get enough of his wickedness." She looked at me guiltily. I paused for a moment before answering.

"I understand why you are attracted to Brian. It's your choice who you end up with. I just worry that Brian will suck all of the goodness out of you like a fucking leech, and then eventually, there will be nothing but darkness." I stroked her face gently.

"I love you; you know. Like I loved my mum," she said, sniffling. I cradled her like a child.

"SSSHH it's OK love. You'll make the right decision, I'm sure you will. You are an amazing girl. I can't pretend I wouldn't want you and Adam to be together. I know he loves you, and even though myself and him do what we do, there is goodness inside. Sounds contradictory, but it's true. We can't deny what we are, but to each other and those around us, we behave accordingly. Argh look at us, all dewy eyed like idiots! Come on now, you need to get some rest." I tucked Melody in and made my way downstairs, fighting back tears. It was only when I got to my car and sat at the wheel that I let go and the tears came.

Finally, it was the eve of Brian's opening. The club

was speckled with candles, flickering and casting eerie shadows on the occupants of the cages. A couple of them made my stomach turn. In one, a thin, pregnant girl in a PVC French maid outfit was huddled up, holding a baby and in another two babies were tucked up in a Moses basket. I was terrified to think what was going to happen to them. The main lighting was turned down to a subdued orange glow, invoking the feeling of the forbidden, of sex and eroticism.

I was dressed in a knee length red PVC wiggle dress, that showed off my cleavage provocatively, my hair piled in ringlets on top of my head. Brian had bought the dress for me as a welcome to the team kind of gesture. He was visibly agitated as he checked his phone, annoyed at the lack of response from someone. Paul behind the bar poured us all a straight vodka, "Here's to making our mark and being the most diabolical sex club in the land!" He said, as we clinked glasses. He looked very submissive in a leather cap with no top and a pair of rubber shorts. He was hot. In other circumstances, I would have been thinking about getting my jollies, but this impending sense of doom just wouldn't leave me. Brian looked dashing in a suit with his top few shirt buttons open, hinting at his muscular chest.

Brian shook off his agitation, "Let's open the doors," he said, his white eyes burning, making the hairs on the back of my neck stand on end. I could see why Melody couldn't keep away. His sense of menace was enticing. The proverbial bad boy. Except with this one you'd be likely to leave in a body bag.

The clients filtered in, dressed in their evening best, the opulence and sheer expense of their ensembles made even me, a woman of means, dizzy. The uber rich. Women with porcelain smiles and men who were withered beyond belief with a gold digger dolly bird on their arm, who probably had frig all idea of what was about to occur this evening.

The music hummed melodically in the background as everyone got comfortable and I served champagne in black flutes.

"Welcome to The Black Rose," said Brian, standing in the middle of the club, his eyes taking in the eager, hungry expressions of his minions. "Tonight, nothing is off limits. You can do what you want, with whomever you want and be as depraved as you want. I want you all to delve deep into your darkest desires and fulfil them here." There was a rumble of applause as he grabbed a flute off my tray, downed the contents, smashed the glass and stabbed his palm, squeezing the blood into his mouth. "Let's cut!!" he yelled and instructed me to help him see to the clients.

I went into the walk-in fridge, the smell of the eyeless, decaying girls, hung by their wrists, dressed in PVC French maid outfits, nearly made me vomit. I wheeled the gurney under the one that was the most putrefied. Half of her face had rotted, and the skin had turned a greenish hue. Her teeth were exposed, and her blonde hair hung wispy and thin down her back, the little maids hat pinned on, covered in specks of dried blood. I cut the rope and she fell awkwardly onto the gurney. I wheeled her out to the thin pale man and his handsome son. Their eyes lit up at the site of the corpse.

The man had eyes like a lizard, slanted and emotionless. He quickly undressed and rammed his thin, veiny cock into the dead girl's mouth. Foul smelling, black liquid pumped out with each thrust, the putrid remains of her decomposed organs. Flies miraculously appeared, landing on his naked body and buzzing around his gore covered cock. His son was wanking his thick, stumpy dick, watching his dad in action.

"The dead never say no son. They are welcoming and reveal their insides to you. I adore the taste of a rotting cunt. Squashy, messy and irresistibly sweet." With that the man spread the girl's swollen legs, lifted her tattered skirt, and started eating her pussy, black goo dripping off his chin, his hand choking his cock to the brink of an orgasm. The boy climbed onto the gurney and began fucking the girl's eye socket. Her face began to collapse as he pounded the decomposed flesh into mulch, bits of brain and rotten skin splattering to the floor and staining his dick. They asked me for another body, a bit fresher, and sat naked with stonking erections whilst I wheeled the remnants out back. Brian had dug a big pit behind the club to throw the dead into. Once the party was over, we were going to pour petrol on it and burn the corpses.

I fetched another dead girl from the fridge, this one newly killed, the cut in her neck swollen and red where she'd been slashed. I left the men to their devices as I was called over by a group dressed in robes and wearing death masks.

"We're ready for her now," a male voice said, so I went to the cage and unlocked it, telling the pregnant girl to hand me the child. I gently put the child back into the cage, wrapping it in a blanket. She came willingly, realising that there was no escape.

"There are more like me, more in that house," she whispered as she lay down on the oval bed. I had no clue what she meant, but knew I had to find out.

The robed figures swarmed around her, chanting a demonic sounding refrain in unison, then one of them produced a sacrificial blade and plunged it into the girl's swollen stomach. She screamed and her head fell to the side, her hazel eyes pleading with me, "Save us!" she said, as the blood bubbled out of her mouth, and she perished along with her unborn child. I felt the bile burning my throat. The figures fell onto the corpse like hungry wolves, biting, tearing and chewing, eating the girl and her baby. The blood spilled onto the floor, filled with bits of skin, gristle and bone.

Everywhere you looked, there was something grisly going on. It was like a demented orgy in hell. The people here were sicker than the clients who came to The Blood Rooms. I felt almost vanilla. I saw the man and his son had cut up the other body into pieces, the father had made a makeshift sex doll. He was holding the hacked off crotch of the girl and ramming it onto his son's hard cock, whilst the exposed femur from the girl's leg was hanging from his arse like a horrific oversized butt plug. Brian was stood at the bar, sipping on a glass of whiskey, naked. An older woman was topless on her knees sucking his cock. Every so often he grabbed her by the hair and forced her to take him deeper.

"How come you have to hurt babies," I said, lighting a cigarette.

"What, too hardcore for you Kendra?" He moaned as he shot his load into the woman's mouth. I shook my head. "Babies make us the most money, and I can get plenty more," he smiled and smacked the woman on her arse as she walked away. I stumped out my cigarette and excused myself, clearing tables amongst bodies that were fucking and covered in viscera.

A beautiful woman in a full-length purple dress sat on the floor holding the baby I'd just put back into the cage. Her big sapphire and gold earrings twinkled, and the baby gurgled trying to grab them. She opened the door to the microwave that was plugged in next to her, put the child inside and turned it on. My insides were screaming; I kept thinking about my baby. What would I have done if this was my daughter? The baby imploded as the microwave dinged. The woman opened the door, scooping out handfuls of gloopy flesh and eating it, not caring if it spilled onto her chest, but lost in the throes of unbridled torture. I needed to go outside and compose myself. I knew I had to save the other babies.

On my way out, Brian grabbed me by the wrist and pulled me into the fridge, pushing me hard over the gurney and lifting up my skirt. He pulled my thong to the side and fucked me hard. The bodies of the dead girls swung rhythmically overhead as he forced his girth into me. I bit my lip, wanting him dead.

"That bitch thinks she can ignore me!" he rasped "She's mine! He can't have her. I will take her. Next time she won't be leaving…" I knew then that Melody was in danger. Brian shot his muck into me and then gleefully began piling the last of the bodies onto the gurney. I pulled my dress down, feeling used and disgusting.

Outside, everyone was either being fucked or eating raw flesh and Brain tipped the last of the bodies onto the floor, the clients in their primal state descending onto them like infected zombies, pulling them to bits. The air was filled with the sound of orgasms and the chomping of guts. I wheeled the gurney to the cage with the Moses basket in and, seeing Brian occupied with his dead I put the babies on it under a sheet next to the bludgeoned torso of a girl and wheeled them outside. I left the gurney next to the pit, the babies had started whimpering, so I separated the nipples from the torn skin and put one in each of their mouths like a gruesome dummy of flesh. The crying stopped. I went into the office to get my bag and text Dario. It was now or never with that fucking filing cabinet. I got my pen knife out of my bag and gently put it into the lock. After some wiggling about, I heard a click and gratefully slid the drawers open. Inside were photocopies of girls with their IDs and, what looked like profiles almost, of babies, with chilling descriptions like, My name's Beatrice and my innocent flesh is ripe for slaughter. I became angry. On each of them was a bank account for payment received with the same address. I took a screen shot. This must be what the pregnant girl was talking about. Were all of these girls here? Fuck! Brian would be jailed forever if the police saw all of this shit.

I closed the filing cabinet and went back outside. The party eventually began to wind down and I diligently deposited all of the remnants of bodies into the pit and began cleaning up, the clinical smell of disinfectant a welcome change from that of rot.

Brian poured petrol into the pit and flicked a lit cigarette onto the pile. It lit with a powerful *Whoosh* and then the air was filled with the acrid smell of burning flesh.

"You did well tonight Kendra," he said, staring into the flames. "Now get yourself home and I'll call you in a couple of days."

Once I got home I lay in a bubble bath for over an hour, happy to get a text off Dario that the babies were washed and fed and with Adam's housekeeper. Tomorrow Adam was going to take them to the police station and say he found them abandoned, which was sort of true I suppose. I drifted off into a troubled sleep, knowing something bad was coming.

8 THE BLOOD ROOMS REVISITED

I stood in front of the full-length mirror, frowning at the pink shadows of whip marks still staining my skin. Adam said no one would notice them, but I could fucking see them. Oh well, I'd be covered in blood soon enough. I was of course, dressed to arouse and excite, wearing a cup less crotchless body suit and black nine-inch patent sandals. My hair was twisted up onto my head.

I needed a drink. I was a bag of nerves tonight, perhaps because it was my first gig since Adam had benched me for nearly two weeks, or because of what Kendra had told us about Brian's party. I couldn't believe he tortured babies. That was sick even for our rotten appetites. The rescued babies had been dropped off at the police station, anonymously of course, and at least they would now have a chance at life and not end up in some shit head's stomach. Kendra had been visibly shaken and not the same upbeat, confident person we knew. She had done her part for the Blood Rooms party though and procured all of the meat we needed for the clients.

I stood on the landing, seeing Priscilla leaving Bridget's room, where she had kissed goodnight to Alice. She flung her arms around me.

"I'm so excited Melody!! I've never been to a party like this before! I'm so glad Ellis can be there with me," she said, animatedly. She looked so grown up for a sixteen-year-old, dressed in a short, tight, black dress and over the knee socks. "Wait till you see your surprise!" she winked at me and skipped down the stairs, her brown hair flowing behind her.

Adam came upstairs then, looking fucking mouthwatering, his tight pants showing the outline of his big cock. We hadn't fucked since the rape. I had been too sore, and I kept waking up in the night dripping with sweat, having night terrors. I suppose all what I'd been through lately had to materialise itself sometime. He was adamant to investigate the address that Kendra had found, but I told him to leave it for now and get our party over with.

"Fuck! You never cease to amaze me. You always look outstanding. Are you ready for your surprise?" I nodded and followed him downstairs. Once we got to the top of the stairs leading to the basement, he put a lace blindfold on me. Fuck I remember the last time my eyes were covered. Thinking of Brian hurt me. I had begun to hate him, but I still wanted his cock. He was different when he was with me, or maybe I'd just been blinded by desire. I pushed all thoughts of him out of my fucked-up head, for now. I was struggling to navigate the stairs blindfolded, so Adam picked me up and carried me the rest of the way. I could hear the crowd's chatter come to a hush and heard the mumbled pleas of frightened victims.

"Do you remember what you told me you thought of the day you auditioned at Enchant?" Adam said into my ear.

"Yes!" I laughed, "dancing in raining blood under decapitated bodies!"

"Well, now you can do it for real." Adam removed the blindfold. Hung from the ceiling by their ankles with their hands bound and tightly gagged, were six bodies, both men and women, totally naked, ready to make it rain blood. I was speechless, fuck me, talk about making your fantasy a reality. I kissed Adam tenderly.

"Go get 'em!" he said as Kendra pressed play. The music pumped through the speakers, the restrained trembling in fear. *"There will be blood, you're gonna die. You'll never make it, never make it through the night…"*

I started to dance feeling all eyes on me. I

unclipped my hair and shook it out suggestively, feeling completely back at home and in my element. All the nerves I'd had upstairs had fluttered away. Adam handed me a gardening scythe and I erotically thrust my pussy to the audience and slit the waiting throats, decapitating one of them by accident. The head rolled and stopped at Cesar's feet. He kicked it away, enraptured by my performance. The blood showered all over me. Shit, the reality was much better than my fantasy. I was covered in scarlet haemoglobin, and I opened my mouth, tasting the mixture of everyone. I raised my hands to the ceiling, feeling the drops hit them, my blood rain. My pussy was so wet. I felt like my body was going to burst into flames from being so aroused. The blood slowed to a dribble, and I lay down in the warm pool of it, fingering my gash. Gladys came over and fell to her knees, not caring that the blood was soaking into her expensive dress. She began tonguing my blood covered cunt.

"Melody I can't get enough of your juicy twat. It is even more delectable when your juice is mixed with blood," she said, grabbing my hips and burrowing her tongue in deeper. For once she didn't make me vomit. I think I was so horny it didn't matter whose tongue brought me to orgasm. Pablo and Bartolomé were grunting and groping my tits, licking the blood off the nipples. I could feel my orgasm building, and it came to a crescendo, my cunt juice filling Glady's mouth. She gulped it down eagerly. I could see a couple of the other clients openly wanking off watching us. I found that so sexy. I stood up, giving each of them a bloody kiss on the cheek.

"We want you to join us in our room baby," said Pablo, grabbing my blood-stained arse.

"Of course. I'm just going to shower," I said, totally not fucking wanting to go near them again and feeling disgusted with myself for letting an old crone and two shit heads make my cunt cum.

I saw Priscilla looking perturbed as Cesar was stood at the bar talking to her and leering. I could see Gladys looking ravenously at Tao languishing in his booth, who was completely uninterested and staring at Ellis sat at the end of the bar. Kendra began cleaning the pool of blood up and cutting the bodies down ready to take to the incinerator.

"Are you sure you're OK?" I said, concerned.

"I'll be fine love. It was just a shock, but I'm getting over it. Go and get yourself cleaned up. The clients will be clamouring for you shortly." I walked towards the shower and Priscilla called me over, as Cesar and the boys went to their room.

"I really can't stand fucking Cesar," Priscilla said, her grey eyes flashing. "He makes my skin crawl. He seemed very interested in Alice and his eyes lit up when I said she was asleep upstairs."

"No one's gonna hurt Alice Priscilla. He's just a dirty old cunt and will be back on a flight to Cuba next week thank God," I said, feeling the blood going stiff on my skin.

I eventually got to the shower and stood under the steaming water, soaping myself up and rinsing the blood away. I felt Adam's familiar hands around my waist and his erect cock nestling between my arse cheeks.

"You look so fucking sexy dancing in blood," he breathed and slid his pulsing dick into me, nibbling my neck and fingering my clit. I screamed as I climaxed and felt his jism dribble down my legs.

"Thank you for the thoughtful gift," I said as I slipped on a backless mini dress.

"It was my pleasure to see your face," Adam said, dressing. I put some lipstick and mascara on and went back to it.

Dario. He loved my deepthroat technique. I knocked on the door to his room and went in. He was stood naked aside from his leather ankle boots. On the table was a teenage girl dressed in a slutty sailor outfit.

"You can fuck my tight pussy if you want to," she said, trying to act all brave and brassy. I wondered if Kendra actually had to sedate her to get her here or just offer her drugs and alcohol. She had no idea that she wouldn't be leaving this place.

"Your pussy looks too good not to fuck," Dario said, shoving his dick inside her. "Fuck, young cunt feels so good squeezing my prick," he mumbled as he roughly fucked her. She thrust her pussy against him, appearing to enjoy herself.

"Melody open my cheeks and rim my arse would you?" I got on my knees and encircled his rusty bullet hole with my tongue, dipping it inside every now and then. He shivered with pleasure.

"Fuck your tongue is magical. Now can you pass me that sander?" I handed him a cordless sander from the counter and her flicked it on to maximum, plunging it into the girl's unwitting face. Her moans of ecstasy were now replaced with muffled cries of anguish. Ears and bits of shredded skin fell to the floor and the blood coated half of the room. Dario noisily ejaculated into her. There was no face left, just a skull surrounded by ground up flesh and blood matted hair. Dario licked the last remains of flesh from the skull.

"Suck my spunk from her cunt Melody and spit it into my mouth," he said, touching his raw cock. I did as I was told. "MMM I love snowballing," he said, smiling. I left him cutting up the girl's body and putting the organs in tubs.

I saw Derek and he beckoned me into Tao's room. A young man was strapped to the table and Tao was sodomising him with a metal pipe, whilst chewing on his sawn-off penis like it was a hot dog sausage. I couldn't understand why Tao was still fully clothed. Derek lopped his dick out and got me to go to work on it, making me give him a sloppy BJ till the spit ran down my chin. He then shoved his cock into the youth's slack mouth that was dribbling out bloody saliva. Tao removed his earbuds.

"Melody, will you stamp on his ribcage with your stilettos and cave his chest in?" Tao said smiling, his fangs glinting chillingly in the overhead lights.

"I should be able to do that. Derek, help me up." Derek pulled out his cock that was still blood engorged, and gallantly held my hand as I climbed onto the table. I stamped as hard as I could hearing a squelch like when you tread in dog shit. The blood pooled around my heel and Derek held my hands to steady me as I rammed my foot in, full force. I heard his ribs crack and then I pierced something soft. His lungs. The blood flowed quickly now, running off the sides of the table. I got down and Tao was pulling open the cavity, chewing on young male insides. Derek handed me a glass of champagne. I drank it in one gulp. Derek cut off the lad's head with a bone saw letting the blood spill over his cock as he wanked himself off, squirting his load into the guy's severed throat.

Tao asked me to take the corpse away and to fetch Ellis. Derek excused himself, throwing Tao a knowing look and headed for the shower room. I wheeled the trolley to the incinerator and flung the body in, then went to the bar. Ellis and Priscilla were snogging passionately. Adam was sitting in a booth sipping his whiskey. He smiled when he saw me, and I couldn't wait to finish and have him make us an omelette. I was starving. Kendra was mixing cocktails behind the bar, and she called me over and poured us a shot. I was relieved that she seemed more like herself.

"Hey Ellis, if you can prise yourself away from Priscilla, Tao wants some coke in his room," I said, playfully.

"MMM we will carry this on later baby," said Priscila, groping his cock as he walked away. "Melody, do you think I could stay over tonight? I don't want to wake Alice to take her home,"

"'Course you can. There's plenty of space. I'm sure we can make up the guest room for you," I said, walking past Gladys' booth, where she was snorting lines off the table.

"Don't forget to come and find me later. I want my cunt eaten," she said, crudely.

I headed for Cesar's room, my nerves gnawing at my stomach, like I had a sixth sense that something extremely fucking bad was going to happen. My gut was always fucking right unfortunately.

I knocked on the door and heard Cesar telling me to come in. Inside looked like a slaughterhouse. A girl, or what was left of her, lay on the table. She had been hacked up and dismembered. Body parts and organs were strewn all over the floor. Pablo grabbed me. Putting a gun to my head.

"What the fuck?! Haven't you already been reprimanded for threatening me with a gun?" I spat.

"Si, they have been cautioned," Cesar said, his voice sickly sweet, "but I need to make sure your lover will do what I ask and what better way to get him to cooperate than to threaten his beloved? Now, call Adam in here." Pablo guided me halfway down the hallway, his gun jabbed painfully into my back.

"Adam, can you come to Cesar's room?" I called.

"Be right there," I heard him answer and wished to fucking God I could rip this fucking cunt's face off, but alas, torture tools were redundant in a gun fight.

Back in the room, the table had been cleared and the girl's body thrown to the floor. I was then flung onto the table and tied tightly with cord. Here we go again. Fuck's sake I was like the poster girl for bound damsels in distress. Bartolomé pointed a pistol at the door and Pablo lifted my skirt and shoved a gun up my cunt. Again. Fuck.

Adam came in and blanched when he saw the scene.

"Cesar why is Melody tied up?"

"Adam, I want you to go upstairs and bring me that

baby, or Pablo will blow your slut's cunt off, and they will fuck her as she's bleeding out," he said, his eyes black and empty.

"I thought we were friends! I've been good to you!" Adam wailed. I was tied so tight I couldn't fucking get free, and I jostled about, but stopped when Pablo rammed his cold piece further into me.

"We are friends. And friendship between businessmen means more than your relationship with this whore. Putas like her are plentiful, but you do this for me, and I guarantee I will make it worth your while. The contacts I can get you now I have my finger in this gangland pie with be beyond your wildest dreams," he chuckled, and I could see Adam's nostrils flare. He looked at me and left the room. Ten minutes later I heard the shrieking of Priscilla. The door opened and Adam came in carrying Alice. Priscilla, snarling like a wild cat tried to pull her from his arms, but Cesar floored her with a punch to the face. Bartolomé threw Adam into the hall, and I could see Bridget lingering outside with her rollers in wearing her nightie, her face tear streaked. Bartolomé locked the door and restrained Priscilla, who was groggily coming round.

"Ellis!!!! ELLIS!!!" Priscilla screamed, but he didn't come. Cesar held Alice and was looking at her with a mixture of arousal and hunger, like an anaconda would size up its meal.

"Get your filthy fucking hands off my baby!" Priscila

yelled. Bartolomé shoved his gun into Priscilla's mouth. She began whimpering. Alice was screaming her little lungs out. I shut my eyes, praying for the miracle that wouldn't come. The screaming stopped and I could hear the tearing of skin, the breaking of bones, Cesar orgasming and Priscilla vomiting. Adam was brutally banging on the door. I opened my eyes and saw the horrendous picture of Cesar chewing and wiping his mouth as he bit the flesh off Alice's arm and swallowed it. There wasn't much left of her, the poor mite.

Priscilla, blazing with anger and overcome with grief, elbowed Bartolomé in the stomach and he dropped the gun. She grabbed it and charged at Cesar, shooting him fatally in the head. He dropped the baby and fell to the floor, dead as fuck. Pablo yanked the gun out of my sore quim and fired a shot. Priscilla dived to the ground, but the bullet had caught her in the shoulder. She aimed her gun and shot Pablo in the gut. He fell against the wall and slid down it leaving a bloody streak. Adam managed to finally kick the door open, and I felt fucking useless, pulling in vain at my restraints. Bartolomé lunged at Priscilla, but she scurried out of the way and shot him in the leg.

"Coño!!!!" he howled and dragged himself along, trying to grab her. Adam kicked him in the face and untied me. Priscilla grabbed an ice pick off the medical trolley and jumped onto Bartolomé, stabbing his eyes and face, he howled in pain and swatted at her, but in her feral state her strength was almost superhuman. She kept slashing him until there was no face left. Adam pulled her off him.

"Don't you fucking touch me! I trusted you, both of you, and you let him eat my baby!!!" Priscilla dropped to her knees and cradled the remains of Alice, rocking as she cried and singing a lullaby. She stood up, still carrying the slaughtered child.

"Ellis!! Where the fuck is he!?" she exclaimed.

"He was in Tao's room," I said, knowing sorry was the most inappropriate thing ever to say at this point.

Bridget was still stood outside in the hall and threw up when she saw Alice's remains.

We all went to Tao's room and Adam knocked. No one answered so he opened the door and saw Tao naked and dickless, squatting over Ellis and riding his hard cock. Ellis had been tied to the table and gagged.

"Oh, my fucking God!" cried Priscilla and fainted, dropping what was left of Alice. She had lost a lot of blood. Kendra came up the hall, wondering what all the commotion was about.

"Fuck me! What's happened?" she said.

"You and Bridget get Priscilla upstairs. She's been shot. I need your nurse skills," Adam said, and the women carried Priscilla away, trying not to look at the dead baby or the spectacle through the open door of Tao's room. Tao saw Adam and I then and took out his buds. He smiled, fulfilled and slid Ellis' cock out of his arse, Ellis' spunk running down his thighs. He then untied him and thanked him for the pleasure, handing him a wad of notes. Ellis stood up embarrassed and then angry.

"Yo, I told you I was no bum boy," he said, punching Tao in the jaw. Tao laughed, spitting out blood.

"You say you aren't gay, but your penis liked the inside of my arse and left it's love juice."

Ellis scowled and left the room, intent on getting to Priscilla.

"I really wish you hadn't raped my dealer Tao," Adam said, sounding pained.

"I had to have him Adam. That itch is finally scratched, and I can assure you I won't go near him again for the rest of my stay."

We left Tao's room and Adam began to shut down the party, telling the guests they would be reimbursed with extra product due to the inconvenience of finishing early. As she left, Gladys licked my cheek.

"I'll be seeing you soon Melody, really soon." With that she doddered upstairs.

Adam and I cleaned up and disposed of all the bodies. No one would ever find Cesar and his cronies luckily.

A few hours later, I was sat in the lounge with Kendra and Adam. Kendra had removed the bullet from Priscilla's shoulder and set her up in the guest room. Ellis had refused to leave her side and had fell asleep sat next to the bed, holding her hand. Kendra had also given Bridget a sedative to calm her down and put her to bed.

"Fuck! I couldn't let them hurt you Melody. I know it was fucking despicable what I did, but I just couldn't lose you. Not now. Not ever," Adam said, sipping his whiskey. I was speechless and drank the Irish coffee Kendra had made me. The thought of having an omelette long gone.

"That Cesar was definitely more suited to Brian's club than ours," mused Kendra, inhaling on her cigarette deeply.

Suddenly there was screaming and ranting upstairs. Priscilla flew down the stairs followed by Ellis who was telling her she should be in bed. She burst into the lounge.

"You killed my baby you cunts! I hate you all!!" Kendra tried to calm her. "You know what Kendra, you're the only one I don't hate, but you're collateral damage. And you," she said to Ellis pointedly, "You can fuck off as well! Putting your dick in his arse!"

"Come on now 'Cilla, you know I ain't no bum boy. You're my girl. He tied me up and forced me," soothed Ellis.

"Then how come you were hard!" Priscilla said, her voice raising an octave. She left the house and Ellis was dogging her steps, apologising and trying to explain himself.

The three of us looked at each other. We didn't realise that a second battle was coming that would usurp the last one. I rolled my eyes wearily and drained my coffee cup.

9 THE BREEDER HOUSE

A couple of days later, I finally got round to setting up my new phone, only to be greeted by a million fucking messages from Brian. Worried and concerned at first, but then aggressive and downright insulting. He had never spoken to me in that tone before. What a cunt.

Kendra said she had to go to The Black Rose for a pow wow with Brian, and that was when she planned on handing her notice in, itching to get back to her stripper mamma duties and some kind of normalcy.

Adam and Dario were planning on staking out the address Kendra had found before planning their attack. Tao had offered to help as an apology for his escapade with Ellis.

Priscilla hadn't turned up for work for the past few

shifts and had also been ignoring Ellis' calls. He figured she just needed time to grieve and get her shit together.

I phoned Brian who was happy to hear from me and remorseful when I told him what had happened. I agreed to meet him, my pussy annoyingly wet at the thought of his dick filling it. I knew this had to be the final time we fucked, even though I'd said this to myself last time. There were facets of his personality that I fucking hated. It seems the charming façade that had bewitched me was beginning to crack. I felt like I was waking up from a torture filled sex dream to realise that the reality I had with Adam was better than being lost to the abyss. We agreed to meet in our usual spot, I slipped out of the house unnoticed; the boys were in the kitchen discussing Brian's demise.

Strangely, Brian was accompanied by Paul. "Are we having another threesome?" I asked as Brian pulled me too him, looking at me like he did that first night we met. Ravenous and primal.

"Something like that," he said, and I was hit over the head from behind and the darkness seduced me into her chilling embrace. This abduction shit had to stop. I needed to put myself under house arrest.

When I awoke, I was in an elegant pink paisley bedroom. The furnishings looked like the décor of a country house, with heavy swag velvet curtains and a mahogany dressing table. The bed had a fancy metal headboard and, as I groggily came round, my head banging, I realised I was cuffed to the bed. I heard familiar cursing next to me and saw that Priscilla was also handcuffed to a matching bed. She was desperately trying to break free. She had a black eye, and I could see the wound on her shoulder had been bleeding. I wiggled my wrist, but the cuffs were on tight and there was no way I was breaking this headboard. Priscilla turned when she heard me.

"Hey," she croaked, "look I'm still seething about what happened. I have been crying for hours about Alice, but that's not going to bring her back is it? I realise that it's not really your fault. You were in the crosshairs of the situation Adam had got himself into. You can't help that he loves you. I'm also fucking angry with Ellis. I think I'm gonna stay away from men for a while." She gave up trying to break the cuffs.

"Fuckin' hell Priscilla. It's OK to grieve. You are allowed to be human. So, How did you get here?" I asked.

"I went to Brian's club, desperate to get revenge for what happened by working for the enemy. He agreed to let me work the bar with that Paul guy and we all had a drink to welcome me into the fold. Next thing I started feeling dizzy and as he grabbed me I fought him off and ended up getting punched, hence my bruised eye. When I woke up, I was here."

The bedroom door swung open, and Brian came in.

"Ah, you're both awake. Excellent." He uncuffed us and put an electronic anklet on each of our ankles.

"What the fuck!" I said, incredulous.

"Calm down baby. Nowhere is locked to you, you are free to roam, but if you go out of the perimeter, then this device will activate, and you will be injected with a lethal dose of cyanide. Priscilla, you will be expected to bear children and be responsible for their care until I have need of them for my clients. My brother will show you around later and introduce you to the other girls."

"Are you serious?!" Priscilla exclaimed, "you cannae keep us prisoner here and breed me to torture my babies. I've already lost one, I'm not losing another."

"What choice do you have?" Brian said flashing that irresistible smile. "You either comply or I kill you now. Your choice." Priscilla shut up and looked at the floor, defeated.

"Melody, you are going to be my woman. You can never leave here. We are going to be together now. No more of this dithering around. Come, let me show you our room." I shot Priscilla a look and her cheeks flushed, and she violently sprung at Brian, her teeth bared. He grabbed her arm.

"Unless you want another black eye, you need to calm down and accept your fate. It really isn't that bad. You are fed, clothed and housed. All you have to do is fuck. And you are a little slut anyway, so that's normal for you." She glared at him; her hands balled into fists.

Brian led me along a meandering hallway. The carpet was dark red and thick, and the walls were adorned with paintings of bygone torture scenes. It was a grand old house and under different circumstances I would've been impressed. He led me up a curved staircase to the third floor. We went through a set of oak double doors to "our" bedroom. It was stunning. Very gothic with a dark wood four poster bed with black silk sheets and black and purple furniture. An opulent balcony overlooked an expanse of lawn and then woods as far as the eye could see. We were in the middle of fucking nowhere. My heart sank, but I knew Adam would find me.

Brian engulfed me in his arms and tried to kiss me. I slapped him, hard.

"MMMM you want it hard; I can do it hard," he said, grabbing my wrists.

"You're just like all the others," I said, down hearted, "I thought you were different."

"My darkness is what drew you in. Give in to me and save all of this heartache. Rule my torture empire with me and be my queen of filth." The hot angry tears came then, and Brian threw me on to the bed, freeing his leaping penis. He lifted my skirt and ripped off my thong, filling me completely. My dim-witted pussy couldn't help but respond to his deep thrusts and I arched my back, moaning in ecstasy as my pussy squirted its sticky cum juice all over him.

Afterwards I was seething with myself. But I knew this was it. I didn't want to be with him.

"Baby don't cry. We are so good together. Succumb to your feelings, then I can take your anklet off." I feigned a smile. "There is a dress for you to wear hung in a dress bag in the wardrobe. Have a bubble bath and relax. Dinner is at 6." He got in the shower, and I ran the bath, adding some bubbles. I sunk into the hot water and exhaled. I pretended to be asleep and felt him kiss my forehead. I just wanted to go home. I no longer felt that I was staying in Adam's house. It was my home, I felt like I belonged. Brian had taken my phone, so I knew I had to find a way to contact Adam. There must be a landline in the place.

I'd soaked in the bath for an hour and then I dried myself and applied some of the perfumed body lotion Brian had left on the dresser. In the drawer was an array of makeup and beauty products. It seemed he had been planning my arrival for a while.

I did my make up dark and edgy. It was my war paint in my battle against these pricks. I opened the bag in the wardrobe. In it was a long, red satin backless dress and matching shoes. Once dressed, I piled my hair on my head. Shit, I looked fucking good. If I was stuck here, I might as well play dress up whilst I looked for an escape route.

I descended the two flights of stairs to the entrance hall, where I was greeted by the butler, who took my arm and led me to the dining room.

"Good evening Melody. I'm Mirfield, the head butler." I nodded, curtly. The dining room was huge, with a long rectangular table and the same country house aesthetic. Brian was sat at the head of the table, and to his right, another handsome man with the same white eyes and long auburn hair. Priscilla was in attendance, along with eight other girls, who were all dressed elegantly and all heavily pregnant. At the other end of the table, a grey-haired woman sat with her back to me. She turned when I entered, and I nearly choked when I saw it was Gladys.

"Ah Melody. I'm so glad you know the truth at last! I have been infiltrating Adam's operation for months, learning about him and the way he runs things, ready to stomp him out. It is time for me and my boys to take over. We also know about Kendra. I saw her at the last Blood Rooms party and then I knew that her working for us was in fact deception. She has since been dealt with." Gladys smiled, with the cunningness of a wolf.

"She's not dead is she?!" I said, alarmed.

"Not dead, not yet. She's in The Black Rose at present; a little tied up!" she laughed, coldly.

Mirfield pulled out a chair to the left of Brian, and I sat down, terrified of what might have become of Kendra. Brian put his hand over mine, and for the first time, his touch made my skin crawl.

"Melody, I'd like you to meet my brother Simon," Brian smiled, and Simon undressed me with his eyes, nodding in approval almost. "And these are our girls, our breeders." Each of the girls looked dead in the eyes, like they had given up hope. I was not going to fucking end up like that.

Dinner was served by girls in PVC French maid outfits dressed like the dead girls in the walk-in fridge. That must be where they end up when they can't birth any more kids. I ate nothing, but the pregnant girls devoured the food like they hadn't eaten in years. None of them spoke. Priscilla violently threw her plate to the floor. It smashed to smithereens, scattering the stew all over the tiles like a splattered turd.

"Fuck this shit! There's no way I'm being shacked up here pumping out bairns for you cunts!" She grabbed her fork and sprung at Brian. Simon grabbed her around the throat.

"Fuck you're a fiery one. I will fuck that out of you don't worry," Simon sneered, and back handed her.

She fell to the ground, out cold.

"Mirfield, take Miss Priscilla back to her room and cuff her. This little slut is going to need a bit of extra discipline brother," Brian said, a lascivious grin on his face. Mirfield carried her over his shoulder and took her back upstairs. I think I'd gone into shock. I felt a bit like a zombie. Everything was going on around me, but I just felt numb.

After dinner, Brian and I retired upstairs. He poured me a whiskey, which I downed in one gulp. He refilled my glass. I took comfort in the lovely, warm, woozy feeling the alcohol gave me when imbibed on an empty stomach. Fuck's sake I had to numb my distress somehow.

Brian caressed my tits, trying to be loving and tender, but the spell was broken. I could see him for what he was now. A monster. He began to finger my cunt and in my alcohol fuelled state, I closed my eyes and thought of Adam. My pussy was soaking instantly, and Brian grunted with pleasure. I heard him rummaging around in the drawer and when I opened my eyes, I saw that he was holding a fucking mummified cock. My eyes widened, and Brian calmed me.

"It's OK Melody. Don't be scared. It's just my dad's dick. I killed him when I was twelve. He was a cunt with my mum, but he was a millionaire. That's how mum got her money. We ate his remains and threw his body in the Thames. Now dad can share in my success and in the pussy of my woman." He shoved the mummified cock into me and his own girthy appendage too, packing my quim tight with two dicks. The skin of the dead penis felt scaly and scratchy. He fucked me for most of the night, getting me to lick my pussy juice off his dad's cock, which made me laugh drunkenly. I couldn't feel much after I'd drank another few whiskeys. I just lay there and let him take me.

Next morning, my body was aching and so was my head. I walked into the hall and heard Priscilla screaming. I ran to her room and opened the door and saw Simon and Brian fucking her, one in her arse one in her cunt. Brian smiled at me and said, "Good morning sexy. You wanna join?" I bristled at the thought, wishing I had a weapon to beat them off her.

"Leave her be. She's had enough," I said, pleadingly.

"I'm nowhere near finished with this whore yet. If you don't like it, get out!" Simon said, angrily.

I left, feeling fucking shit because I just let them hurt her. There was fuck all in the room to fight with. What I wouldn't give for a claw hammer right about now. I heard the familiar, croaky refrain of Gladys having an orgasm. I went to the source of the sound and saw through a partially open door, Gladys sat on one of the pregnant girl's faces getting her cunt eaten, leaning back against the girl's swollen belly. I had to get out of this fucking depraved knocking shop. I went back upstairs and had a look in the bathroom for something, anything that I could use to break the lock of this fucking leg cuff. Elated, I found a pair of tweezers and tried in vain to pick the lock. The tweezers snapped. Frustrated I stalked downstairs.

A while later, I was sat on one of the white metal ornate garden chairs on the terrace drinking a black coffee. Priscilla joined me, her hands shaking as she lit her cigarette. She had been badly beaten, and not only did she have a black eye but also a red mark across the other side of her face and a busted lip. She sat next to me clearly in pain.

"I'm sorry I couldn't help you," I said, guiltily.

"What could you have done? I'm just glad they finally uncuffed me." She took a huge drag of her cigarette. "I can't even have any drugs here. He's only let me smoke because I let him fist me."

We sat in morbid silence then Priscilla said, "I reckon you and I could take these cunts out."

I sat up straight and determined. I'd gotten myself out of several fucked up situations, no matter the odds. I could do it again. I turned to her and said, "I had a walk around the rooms downstairs earlier. The cutlery, kitchen knives, in fact anything that can be used as a weapon is locked away somewhere. All the drawers in the kitchen are empty. We need to find the keys to these anklets. I've looked in mine and Brian's room and the keys aren't there, but I bet Gladys has a set."

Priscilla became excited. "Then we craft some sort of weapon. Leave it to me. I learnt a trick or two when I was on the street."

"OK, so tonight we make our move. I'll come for you just after midnight, then we will ransack Gladys' room, I just hope they don't have guns," I said, knowing full well that we were going to have to fight with everything we had to get out of there alive.

It was just before midnight. I had spent three hours fucking Brian in every position possible and letting him cut my pussy and nibble the open wounds. I was so fucking sore and had put a sanitary pad in my knickers to soak up the blood. But there was no time to dwell on agony. I slipped into Priscilla's room, and she showed me the shiv she had made by melting her toothbrush with a lighter. She was one tough little bitch! Silently we moved down the hall and panicked when we heard old Mirfield patrolling the halls, so we ducked behind a stone statue of a woman being impaled through her cunt and hid in the shadows till the coast was clear. As luck would have it, Gladys' bedroom door was open. We crept in and saw the old cow snoring on her big oval bed, oblivious to what was about to happen. I picked up one of her duck down pillows and held it firmly over her head. She flailed her scrawny body about blindly and I pressed harder, thinking of all the girls she had abused and held against their will. Priscilla viciously slit her throat with the shiv and the blood spurted out, staining the ivory sheets. We tore the room apart, finding nothing but drawers full of sex toys and labelled pen drives of the many girls these pricks had imprisoned. I glanced at the picture on the bedside table of Gladys with Simon and Brian when they were boys. I picked up the picture, wondering how two innocent looking kids could've turned out the way they did. The picture felt abnormally heavy at the bottom, and when I opened the back, there was a key bearing the same name of the company that was emblazoned on our anklet.

"Crafty bitch," whispered Priscilla, as I undid her leg cuff. I picked up Gladys' phone off the nightstand and dialled Adam's number.

"Adam. Don't talk. Just listen. Priscilla and I are in the house that Kendra found the address for. Come and get us and bring back up. There are eight other girls here." I whispered fiercely.

"Melody thank fuck! We've been searching for you for the last two days! I can't take this nearly losing you all the time. I'm going to have to chain myself to your side," he said, laughing inopportunely. "Kendra isn't answering her phone either.."

"No," I said, cutting him off. She's in The Black

Rose. Just hurry and get here."

"I'm on my way, and Melody, don't call the police yet until justice is served." I hung up and stamped on the phone.

"The cavalry is coming, but I still got some of my own revenge to dish out," Priscilla said, grinning fiendishly. We tiptoed down the hall and tried Simon's room. The door was locked.

"Fuck! Don't worry, just follow my lead," Priscilla said, knocking sharply. Simon opened the door bleary eyed, and Priscilla grabbed his cock and murmured, "Oh baby, do you know I've come to like your fat cock in my gash. You wanna fuck some more and have a threesome with us?"

"Yes Simon. Just don't tell Brian," I winked, and he ushered us inside. He lay down on the bed, looking at us expectantly, now fully fucking awake. Priscilla climbed on top of him and began kissing his neck, whilst I wanked off his thick cock, feeling it get harder with each stroke. Priscilla then bit a huge fucking chunk out of his neck and shoved the shiv down his throat as he opened his mouth to cry out. The blood spurted up like a fountain and Priscilla fired the chunk of flesh into his face.

"Cunt!" she said, through gritted teeth and spat a blood filled gozzball at him. We left Simon's room, hoping not to run into wily Mirfield again. We then went into the girl's rooms. Some were locked and we had to knock, but some were open. We undid all of the anklets and took the girls on mass to the lounge downstairs.

"Someone is coming. You will be able to leave this place," I said, as the girls huddled together in the corner.

"We were told they would kill our families if we ever tried to leave," said one of the girls in a frightened whisper.

"You don't need to be scared anymore. Help is coming," I said, reassuringly. As I went to leave the lounge, Mirfield stood in the doorway holding a rifle.

"Going somewhere?" he said smugly, forcing me back into the lounge with his gun. Priscilla snaked behind him only to be stopped by Brian, who plunged his pen knife into her side. She fell to the floor, the blood pooling around her. The girls screamed and grouped tighter together. Brian lifted his hand to hit me, then stopped.

"How could you!!? I love you!" he wailed.

"Love. You don't even know what that means," I said in a faraway tone. Brian wiped his eyes with the back of his hand.

"Mirfield, keep your gun on the girls till I get back. Now Melody, get Priscilla up. We're going to see Kendra." I lifted Priscilla up and she screamed. She was losing a lot of blood. "She's bleeding out Brian.

She needs stitches," I said, pointedly.

"Get her to hold that on it." He threw a cushion at me from the sofa. "Now come on. Get to the car."

We made it out to the courtyard, and I could've cried with happiness when I saw Dario's jeep pull up. Inside joining him and Adam were Ellis and Tao. Dario and Tao ran into the house and Adam walked towards Brian pointing the golden gun gifted to him by Cesar.

"On second thoughts, I want to make you suffer. Shooting you is too easy," Adam growled, dropping the gun to the floor. He dived on top of Brian and started punching fuck out of his face. Brian, not to be outdone, punched Adam in the gut winding him. They rolled around on the floor like two enraged bears, making each other bloodier with each strike. Brian started fighting dirty, biting Adam wherever he could, leaving teeth marks in his cheek. Adam managed to stand and kicked Brian squarely in the fucking head. Brain faltered and fell to his knees. Adam went to deliver the finishing blow, when Brian threw a handful of gravel intro his face. He scuttled away to his car, tearing off down the driveway.

"Fuck are you OK?!" I said, checking Adam's eyes as he wiped the grit out.

"I'm fine," he said, bravely. We heard a gunshot from inside. About five minutes later. Tao and Dario returned.

"The old guy is dead," Dario said.

"OK, well we need to go after Brian. Dario you stay here and call the police. Priscilla, I think you and Ellis better stay here as well. Melody I know you will never stay even if I beg you to," Adam said, holding my hand.

"You've got that fucking right," I agreed.

"If we are going to get Kendra, I'm coming," rasped Priscilla, holding the cushion to her wound.

"If Priscilla's going then I am," Ellis said defiantly.

"OK fuck's sake well come on then," Adam said, and we all piled in the car. Priscilla was spaced out from blood loss.

"Ellis, give me something for the pain," she mumbled, and Ellis gave her a pill. She swallowed it without water. There was something I had to tell Priscilla, even though I knew this was the worst ever time to do it. If she died tonight, I wouldn't want her to not have closure. Perhaps I was a selfish bitch and I just wanted to clear my conscious. Maybe I too was a monster.

"Priscilla, there's something I've been meaning to tell you for a while. Your boyfriend Bill and his friends kidnapped me and hurt me, so I killed them all." Her eyes fluttered open, and I felt strangely unburdened after finally revealing my secret. Ellis looked at me open mouthed saying *fuck* under his breath. We were all silent for the rest of the journey and once we arrived outside of the club, Adam and Tao told us to wait while they checked inside. Tao unsheathed a samurai sword from his cane that I'd seen him have with him since the first time I saw him. Shit, he had been armed with that all along. Ellis held Pricilla up.

"Babe you should wait in the car," Ellis said concerned.

"Do you know how you can make it up to me baby," she drawled, spitting blood, her eyes wild, "kill Melody. Not only has her shag taken my child, but she has killed the love of my life too!!" She pulled Adam's gun from the waistband of her skirt.

"Yo I can't kill Melody. I ain't no killer 'Cilla."

"Unfortunately for you, I am," Priscilla said, and shot Ellis point blank in the face, killing him instantly. I bolted into the club, narrowly missing a flying bullet. I stopped dead when I saw Adam on his knees, sobbing. Hung from the ceiling naked with two hooks through the skin on her back was Kendra. Her arms and legs had been cut off and the wounds cauterized. There was a massive pool of blood underneath her.

"Get her down!" I yelled my eyes brimming over with tears. Her eyes opened slightly. She was barely alive.

"Hiya love," she whispered, her voice barely audible

as I struggled to free her from the hooks. "It's too late for that now. I want you to kill me," she said, knowing her end was near.

"I can't kill you! It's OK, we'll get you fixed," I blubbered. Adam stood up and helped me, but the more we struggled the more her skin tore.

"Stop," she said, a lone tear trickling down her cheek, "kill me and let me feed you. Don't let me die like this." Adam and I looked at each other.

"We love you," I cried, hugging her mutilated body. Adam broke a bottle and rammed it into her chest.

"And I love you," she said with her dying breath.

10 BURN IT ALL DOWN

Adam pulled Kendra's warm heart from her chest, and we both devoured it, crying with each mouthful. Priscilla came barraging into the club, firing off a couple of warning shots, one of which hit Kendra's dead body. Adam and I dived behind the bar. When Priscilla saw Kendra's destroyed body, she began to wail in horror.

"Brian you cunt!!!" she said, blazing with anger, "like to pick on girls do you?! Come and pick on me!! You've already stabbed me but I'm not dead yet! Come out you coward!!"

There was a loud crash, and a ruckus from the back of the club. Priscilla held her side, gritting her teeth and then steadied her nerve and ran into the fray.

"She's gone. Let's look for Brian. There aren't many places to hide in here. It's time we finished him off for good," Adam said, picking up a corkscrew from behind the bar. We checked in the walk-in fridge. No Brian, but two dead girls hung on meat hooks. Both of them looked pretty fresh. One was missing both of her legs; the wounds cauterized just like Kendra's, and the legs plastic wrapped and shelved at the back of the fridge.

Suddenly we heard gunshots. Priscilla must have found Brian. As we left the walk-in fridge, Tao came from the dressing room holding the dripping, severed head of Paul the barman. He flung it on the floor, where it rolled randomly and stopped, Paul's eyes looking straight at me, I shivered, and we headed to Brian's office.

Priscilla was lay on the floor wheezing from being incapacitated by Brian. The office looked like a bomb had gone off. They had obviously been tussling before Brian had put her down. He stood behind his desk, battered and covered in blood, holding a blow torch.

"Come any closer and I'll burn Priscilla and all of you," he snarled.

"I'm going to kill you for what you did to Kendra," Adam said, narrowing his eyes.

"I don't know what I ever saw in you," I said, "I need my head tested. I like my own kind of semi-darkness. You can keep your nothingness. I still want to be human. I don't want to be a villain." Brain laughed icily, "Melody you are a fucking hypocrite! You kill and eat just like me!"

"But we have lines we do not cross," Adam replied, "and we know how to treat people, unlike you. We may be cannibals, but we have a code."

Tao handed Adam the sword. "For Miss Kendra," he said, sombrely. Adam dropped the useless corkscrew and swiped the sword at Brian, but he jumped out of the way and fired the blow torch, so we all ducked. I dragged Priscilla into the bar area. She was chattering inaudibly and moaning. Tao rolled towards Brian and got behind him grabbing his neck and doing some full-on martial arts shit that winded him and made him choke. Tao kicked Brian expertly at the knees, breaking both of his legs. Brian yelled in agony, but then started laughing inanely as Tao grabbed his arms behind his back.

"Go on then!" he chuckled, "do it! Just so you know, Melody loved my fat cock in her. She's been fucking me behind your back for weeks!" I stood in the doorway, my cheeks flushing guiltily.

"I don't fucking care," Adam said, "if she wanted to be with you so bad, then why did she want to escape your breeder house? I think we both know who she chose. Enjoy eternity in darkness- alone." Adam sliced off Brain's head with one blow. The blood spurted up in the air, covering him and Tao.

"He's right, I have been fucking him," I said, sheepishly, "I know I was wrong and I'm sorry. I never wanted to hurt you."

"Who is the one you're standing next to now? Me. I always knew we would be together. Let's get out of here," he said, tiredly. We both gave each other a look that meant more than words. There was so much I wanted to say to Adam as to why I was so attracted to Brian and why I did what I did, but I guess none of it mattered anymore.

Adam picked up the blow torch and went to the bar, smashing bottles and scattering alcohol all over.

"The Black Rose is no more," He said, ceremoniously. I went to fetch Priscilla, but the body was gone. She grabbed me from behind, the gun at my head. I was seriously beginning to hate fucking guns.

"You stupid cunt Melody!" she said, her voice burbling with blood, "pulling me to safety! I never would have done that for you, not after what you've done. Now Adam, watch as I kill her, the way you killed my baby." She was swaying, almost at the point of passing out. I tried to escape, but the anger and grief she had suffered made her hold me fast, even in her weakened state. She pulled the trigger as I elbowed her in the guts and fell to my knees. She missed me, and Adam turned on the blow torch and ignited the alcohol he had spilt all over the floor. There was a loud hiss, and the bar area went up in flames. I leapt out of the way, but Priscilla caught fire and rolled on the floor trying to put herself out amongst the inferno.

We staggered out of the building and then there was a loud bang that sounded like ten thunderclaps sounding all at once. The whole place was now ablaze, the structure falling as the flames devoured it.

My body sagged against Adam, and he gently touched my face and kissed me.

"I love you," I said, and Adam's face brightened, "I think I always did. I just got a bit lost along the way."

Tao started the Jeep, and we got in.

"Let's get out of here and go and pick up Dario before the police arrive," Adam said, as the Jeep sped away, "we can't have them looking into what we all do."

I looked back through the window at the smoke and leaping flames and thought I could've been fucking swallowed by darkness, but I managed to claw myself out.

As we drove down from the hills, Dario now in tow, dawn was breaking.

11 THE SCANDAL

"Isla, this story is going to make you hot property, and for that reason I'm so glad you work for me," said my editor after finishing reading my copy.

"Millionaire Widow Embroiled in Torture, Kidnap and Rape Scandal" read the headline, and I couldn't believe that I, Isla Todd, finally had a front-page story. My hard work had paid off. Now I was going places.

I had interviewed the lead detective who was very forthcoming, especially when I flashed a bit of leg and dropped a few flirty comments. They had found several bodies at the scene who were the perpetrators of the abuse. Eight pregnant girls and two maids were rescued, three of whom had been silenced by having their tongues cut out. On interviewing one of the terrified girls, the policeman was told that they had been made to wear anklets that would inject them with cyanide if they left the grounds. The girl said that a dark stranger had made the call to the authorities. He had made sure they weren't in danger before vanishing into the night.

Now, the girls were in intensive care and their families had been notified. The police had been able to solve several of their missing person cases with the discovery of these youngsters.

In the basement of the house, the police found plastic tubs filled with body parts and some larger containers with the bodies of newborn babies inside in large chest freezers. Swathes of human skin were hung up on hooks, like they had been left to dry out, and there was a room which had clearly been used for torture, with a gynaecologist's bed and a trolley with various instruments of pain on it. The many puddles of blood, some dried up, were being analysed for potential leads on cold cases. Perhaps the most harrowing things to be discovered were the pen drives containing hours of footage of girls being raped and tortured and sometimes eaten. All three members of this wicked family were involved in the horrific acts that occurred. The older son's body is believed to be amongst the smouldering remains of the club the family owned. Police are unsure of how the blaze started and if it was arson, but they are currently picking through the wreckage to see if they can find any more evidence. Behind the club, authorities discovered some disturbed ground that when moved, revealed the skeletons of around fifty people. The bones have been sent away to be evaluated via dental records to ascertain the identity of the victims.

This story has certainly shocked the local community, and people are relieved that justice has